Macbeth and Son

Macbeth and Son

Jackie French

📖 Angus&Robertson
An imprint of HarperCollins*Publishers*

Angus&Robertson
An imprint of HarperCollins*Publishers*, Australia

First published in 2006
by HarperCollins*Publishers* Australia Pty Limited
ABN 36 009 913 517
www.harpercollins.com.au

HarperCollins*Publishers*
25 Ryde Road, Pymble, Sydney, NSW 2073, Australia
31 View Road, Glenfield, Auckland 10, New Zealand
77–85 Fulham Palace Road, London W6 8JB, United Kingdom
2 Bloor Street East, 20th floor, Toronto, Ontario M4W 1A8, Canada
10 East 53rd Street, New York NY 10022, USA

National Library of Australia Cataloguing-in-Publication data:

French, Jackie.
    Macbeth and son.
    For children aged 10–14 years.
    ISBN 978 0 20720 034 2.
    ISBN 0 207 20034 3.
    I. Title.
A823.3

Cover images of boy and warriors © Corbis/Australian Picture Library
All other cover images © Shutterstock
Cover and internal design by Darren Holt, HarperCollins Design Studio
Map by Darren Holt, HarperCollins Design Studio
Typeset in 10 on 14 Bookman by Helen Beard, ECJ Australia Pty Limited
Printed and bound in Australia by Griffin Press on 60gsm Bulky Paperback White

5 4 3 2 1   06 07 08 09

*To Edward, Nöel, Angela, Bree, Emma,
Lisa and Liana, with love and enormous
gratitude. This book would only have been
a shadow of itself without you.*

ALBA
AND ITS NEIGHBOURS
~11th century~

NORWAY

ORKNEYS

MORAY

ALBA (Scotland)

ATHOLL

Scone •

NORTHUMBRIA

IRELAND

ENGLAND

WALES

London •

Prologue

Lulach

Lady Macduff: Yes, he is dead:
    how wilt thou do for a father?
Son: Nay, how will you do for a husband?
       (*Macbeth*, Act IV, Scene 2, lines 38–39)

The noise wailed like the wind, waking him up.
Pipers, thought Lulach, rolling over on the goose-feather mattress. Who was playing bagpipes so late at night? All the pipers had gone with the army, marching at the front when his father had led the men of Clan Moray to this summer's war.

Lulach ran to the window and peered out. It was never quite dark even at midnight on summer nights here in the north. Tonight the cobbles and stone walls of the rath's great courtyard were silver in the moonlight. The blacksmith's anvil gleamed. Lulach could see the river from here, with its ripples of moonlit gold, and the fishermen's cottages by the shore. Up on the hill the sheep bleated at the noise.

Other people were waking up now. Sleepy women hurried from the Hall door, clasping their shawls or cloaks about them. There were even a few men as well, too old to follow their chief to the war. One or two children clutched their mother's skirts. But there were few children in Moray these days. Wars every summer meant starving winters, and children died, even here in the rath — the Hall and clustered cottages of the Mormaer, the Chief.

The pipers were coming closer. The army must be coming back! Maybe they'd won this war, thought Lulach exultantly. King Duncan had led his men to war five times, and lost every one of them. But maybe this time . . .

Lulach thrust his feet into his boots and grabbed his cloak from the chair. It was midsummer, but here in the north of Alba the short summer nights were chilly.

Lulach ran down the stone stairs and out into the courtyard. The people stood aside to let him pass. Lulach was only five, but he was still the Mormaer's son.

Knut was already at the front of the crowd, next to Lulach's mother, the Lady Gruoch. Knut was Lulach's foster brother and best friend, three years older than Lulach. Like most sons of high-born families, Knut was spending several years with another family, to learn their ways and help cement alliances between the families.

'What's happening?' Lulach demanded.

'The army is coming back!' said Knut excitedly.

'But it's night-time!'

The Lady Gruoch glanced at them both. Her face was as pale as her blonde plaits. 'The moon is light enough to show their way,' she said.

There was a note in his mother's voice that Lulach had never heard before. She grabbed his hand, so hard his knuckles hurt.

What was so urgent that battle-weary men would travel at night, with just the light of the moon to guide them? Why didn't the women run to meet the men, as they had last year when the army returned?

Why were they so silent?

Lulach peered up the muddy track. He could see the four pipers now, their bagpipes sobbing more poignantly than any human voices. Six men walked behind them, each helping to carry a bier on their shoulders. There was something lumpy on it, covered with a cloak. Behind them trudged the tired, tattered men of Moray's army.

A hundred men had marched away six weeks ago. Lulach didn't think there were as many as that now.

He tried to make out their faces in the moonlight.

Where was his father? The Mormaer's place was at the front of the army! When they marched away his father had ridden just behind the pipers on his big red horse.

Had the horse been killed in battle?

'My Lady?' It was Meröe. She had been his mother's nurse, and had come with her when the Lady Gruoch married the Mormaer of Moray. Now Meröe was in charge of all the women in the rath — deciding who would make the cheeses, weave the cloth or take the cows to the hills in summer; making sure the fish were dried well enough to be stored and the barley was safe from the mice.

Knut had told him that Meröe was a witch. According to Knut, old women turned into witches

3

when their chins got hairy. Meröe's beard was almost as good as her son's, and her mouth was all wrinkles like an apple after winter.

Knut said witches could kill a cow just by looking at it. But Lulach wasn't frightened of witches.

Much.

'I'll take the boy, my Lady,' said Meröe gently.

The Lady Gruoch nodded. She let go of Lulach's hand. He felt Meröe's horny one grip him instead.

His mother strode over the stones of the courtyard, lifting her skirts to keep them free of grime.

The pipers stopped their playing.

One of the men left his place below the bier and came towards her.

'I'm sorry, my Lady,' he said softly. It was Kenneth, Meröe's son. In peacetime he was Moray's Steward, second only to the Mormaer — in charge of choosing which family would farm which piece of land, and who would crew the fishing boats. In wartime he was the second in command. Before the army went to war, Kenneth had made Lulach pipes from a sheep's bone, and shown him how to call the birds with it.

What's happening? wondered Lulach. Why is Kenneth sorry? Have we lost this war too?

'Let me see him.' Gruoch's voice was calm. Lulach would have thought she felt nothing, if he hadn't seen her eyes as she turned briefly to glance at him.

'My Lady ...' Kenneth hesitated. 'He was badly hurt, my Lady. Burned. Perhaps you shouldn't see him.'

'Let me see him!'

The men lowered the bier.

Suddenly Lulach realised what was happening. The men were carrying a body!

Was that what the silence had meant? That the Hall was mourning for its chief?

No, thought Lulach. No! His father couldn't be dead!

His father was strong! His father could carry a deer slung over his shoulder, and fight two men at once with his broadsword! No enemy could hurt his father!

The Lady Gruoch lifted the cloak and stared down at the body on the bier. Just for a moment her face twisted. Her fist pressed against her mouth, as though to stifle a cry. Then she was in control again. As the men watched she bent forward and kissed her dead husband, then covered him again with the cloak.

The women were moving now, running into the darkness as the men broke ranks, trying to find their husbands, fathers, loved ones. But they all left a small clear space around the six men and the bier.

Lulach wrenched himself from Meröe's grasp and darted forward. But the bier was too high for him to see his father's body.

'Lulach! Go back to the Hall!' His mother's voice was steady. But only just.

'I want to see him!' insisted Lulach. 'I want to say goodbye too.'

'It's the boy's right to see,' said Kenneth quietly.

'He's only five summers old!'

'And one day he'll be a man, and can take revenge on his father's killer. My Lady?'

The Lady Gruoch said nothing for a moment. Then she nodded. 'Let him see,' she whispered.

Kenneth gestured to the other men. They lowered the bier even further. Kenneth pulled the cloth from Lulach's father's face again.

But there was no face.

Lulach stared. There was only black ... and bone ... and charred eye sockets — like a stag's head thrown onto the fire after the dogs had chewed it.

This wasn't his father! It couldn't be!

'They set the watchtower on the cliffs alight. He was burned alive with fifty of our men,' said Kenneth softly. 'That's the work of Thorfinn the Raven Feeder, my lad. Now you know.'

It seemed like the whole courtyard was silent now, watching, waiting. I have to kiss him farewell too, thought Lulach.

The blackened eye holes stared at him. He thought he would be sick.

But he was the Mormaer's son. He bent forward. . .

Closer ... closer ... The skull felt cold against his lips. The stench of burned hair and bone and flesh filled his nostrils.

Then he'd done it. He forced himself not to wipe his lips.

The men picked up the bier again. They began to carry it into the Hall. The body would stay there where all could see it until the burial.

'You should be in bed,' the Lady Gruoch said, then gestured to Meröe. 'Take Lulach upstairs again,' she ordered. She bent down to hug him. 'You did well,' she whispered. 'Try to sleep now.'

Sleep? How could he sleep? Even though the body on the bier was covered, the hollow eyes still seemed to watch him.

Maybe they'll follow me forever, thought Lulach.

Knut tried to speak to him. But Lulach ignored him.

He followed Meröe up the stairs. Once he was in bed she pulled the linen sheet and sheepskin blanket over him. But there was no way he could sleep.

The leading men and women of Moray would be downstairs planning, while their dead Mormaer's body lay on its bier among them.

Who would be Mormaer of Moray now?

New mormaers were elected from the best candidates in the old mormaer's family, just like the mormaers and bishops of Alba elected one of the mormaers to be their king.

But who was left to be the mormaer? So many men had been killed during the seven years that King Duncan had been on the throne. Now there was only Lulach, and he was too young to be elected.

Maybe Mother will be mormaer, he thought. His father had appointed her his tanist before he left for war. Each mormaer appointed a tanist, someone to inherit their position.

Tanists weren't always elected mormaer — that was up to the people — but they usually were. After all, the tanist was given experience and training by the former mormaer that other candidates missed out on. Women could stand for election for both mormaer and king, though few did.

I should be crying, thought Lulach. But no tears came. The dead black thing downstairs wasn't his father. His father was tall, with blond plaits that bounced on his shoulders as he rode. Maybe tomorrow he'd gallop up the track, swing Lulach into the air once more ...

Lulach must have slept again. When he opened his eyes this time the window was pink with dawn.

'Lulach.' The Lady Gruoch sat on the bed beside him, with something in her hand.

Lulach sat up. She's going to say it was a mistake, he thought. He's not dead at all. That thing on the bier was someone else and Father's coming home.

'Here.' His mother handed him a piece of oatcake, spread with honey. It had been months since Lulach had tasted honey, but his stomach felt too tight for food. He nibbled the oatcake anyway, and felt its sweetness fill his mouth. Food was too precious to be wasted.

'Lulach, I have to go away. I'll be gone a sennight, maybe more.'

Lulach swallowed the last crumbs of oatcake. 'Can I come?'

Gruoch shook her head. 'No. I'll travel fastest just with Kenneth.'

'Where are you going?'

His mother bit her lip. 'Lulach ... Moray needs a chief. We can't be leaderless too long, not in times like these. I'm going to ask my cousin if he'll stand for election.'

'But ... but he's not one of Father's family! He can't be mormaer!'

'He's your father's cousin too. And if I marry him, the people will accept him.'

Lulach stared at her. 'You can't marry someone else!'

His mother's face twisted in an almost smile. 'I can, you know. Men fight on the battlefield. Women do their duty in other ways. This is my duty, Lulach.'

'But why can't you be mormaer? You're the tanist.'

She shook her head. 'Your father never intended me to rule Moray for long. King Duncan has started five wars in five years. He plays at war like a dog loves romping in the deer guts after a hunt. There'll be more wars, and more again, as long as Duncan is on the throne.' Her voice was bitter. 'Moray needs a battle leader, not a woman. I'll stand for election too, because that's what people expect. But they'll vote for a man.'

She stood up. 'Be brave, Lulach. This is what your father wanted. We talked about it before . . .' her voice broke just for a moment, 'before he left.' She bent down and hugged him hard.

Then she was gone.

Another mormaer! thought Lulach.

It wasn't right! His father was the mormaer! And he was the mormaer's son!

What will I be when there's a new mormaer? he thought. His stepson . . . not his son.

How could your whole world vanish in a night? His father gone, his position as mormaer's son . . . even his mother would belong to a stranger now.

Perhaps Mother's cousin will say no, he thought. Perhaps he won't want to marry her and be Mormaer of Moray.

But how could any man not want Moray? It was one of the biggest, most powerful lands in all of Alba. Only King Duncan's clan, Atholl, was as powerful.

Suddenly he wanted to sleep again. Not because he was tired, but to escape, to vanish into another world.

When I wake up it will all be gone, he promised himself. Father will be alive. I'll be the mormaer's son again.

Dreams would be much better than this . . .

Lulach shut his eyes tightly. Yes, I'll dream of a different world, he told himself. A safe world. A world without war . . .

Chapter 1

Luke

The time approaches,
That will with due decision make us know
What we shall say we have, and what we owe.
(*Macbeth*, Act V, Scene 4, lines 16–18)

'A world without war,' said Sam.

'What?' Luke stopped gazing out of the limousine window. He still felt embarrassed riding in the back with Sam while no one was in the front with the driver. 'Sorry, I was thinking about something else.'

'A world without war,' repeated Sam patiently. 'That's what I said on my show this morning. When I was a kid I dreamed about a world without war. That's why I did International Relations at uni.'

'Love your show, Mr Mackenzie,' the driver said over his shoulder. 'Watch it every day if I'm not working.'

'Hey, I just try to tell people the truth. But thanks, mate. You know, that's what President Clinton said to me last time I interviewed him. Great bloke, Bill Clinton — you'd really like him. He said to me, "A democracy depends on letting people know what's really happening.'" Sam gave his 'being friendly to the public' grin.

Sam's 'being friendly to the public' grin was different from his real grin. Sam didn't give his real grin often, but when he did it reached his eyes. But the driver didn't know this. Luke could almost see him swell with pride at meeting someone who'd talked to an ex-president.

He glanced at Sam's eyes again. Sam's eyebrows were still slightly darkened from the TV make-up, and his eyelashes looked dark too.

Luke wondered if the driver would think Sam was so wonderful if he heard the way Sam talked about the viewers at home, back in Biscuit Creek. 'The punters', he called them. 'Got to give the punters some blood for their bucks,' he'd said last week, when Mum had complained about seeing those kids' bodies on breakfast TV. And Mum hadn't argued with him at all, as if anything Sam said had to be okay.

Sam looked at his watch. 'Soon be there.'

'Yeah. Right,' said Luke. He stared out the window again at the passing Sydney suburbs. It all seemed so cramped. No paddocks, no bush. You couldn't even see the horizon here. The houses were too close together, as though their gardens had all shrunk. If he made it into St Ilf's Grammar School he supposed he'd be seeing suburbs like these every day. Or did boarders have to stay at school all the time?

But there was no way he'd pass this entrance exam, he told himself. Dumb old Luke. 'Pity he doesn't have his stepfather's brains,' he'd once heard Mrs Easson say to another teacher. 'He tries hard, but ...' and then she'd seen him listening, and stopped.

He was going to flunk this big-time. But at least Mum and Sam would be pleased he'd tried.

He hoped they'd be pleased, anyway — even when he bombed. St Ilf's was Sam's old school. He and Mum had gone to Breakfast Creek Central, where Luke was going now. But then Sam had won a scholarship down to St Ilf's, gone on to uni and become rich and famous, and Mum had stayed at Breakfast Creek and married Dad and worked on the farm.

She hadn't met Sam again till after Dad died, when Sam came back for their school reunion. Mum had come home all gooey and dreamy, and within a year they'd got married and Sam had moved in, and he'd had a stepfather ...

... and things had changed ...

'Here we are,' said Sam, as the limo swung through the gates. They were stone, with something written in Latin and a crest carved on them.

Luke peered ahead. He could see tall trees that looked like they'd been there forever, and the sort of grass that was regularly mowed and watered, and flower beds all around, as if no one at St Ilf's had ever heard of a drought — a far cry from the rutted dirt playground and shabby weatherboard buildings of Breakfast Creek Central.

I'm going to fail, I'm going to fail, thought Luke. There was no way he'd ever pass an entrance exam in a place like this, no matter how much coaching Sam had arranged for him and how many old exam papers he'd gone through.

Sam was out of the door before the driver could open it for him. Luke followed him up the steps. A crowd of boys and parents were already milling around on the grassy terrace.

More flowers, thought Luke. There was enough grass here to feed all of Mum's cattle for a month.

Maybe if he did end up going to school here he could send the grass clippings home.

No one else was wearing boots and moleskins. Luke wished he'd worn the expensive joggers Sam had given him last month. Most of the boys seemed to have both parents with them too. For a moment he wished Mum had come as well. She wouldn't have looked out of place these days, not with her hair all short and streaked like most of the other mums here — not if she dressed in her 'going to Sydney' clothes, anyway, and remembered to do her hair.

But he'd been so sure he was going to flunk he'd asked her not to come. And Sam had agreed. 'Gives us boys a chance to spend some quality time together,' Sam had said.

Luke supposed 'quality time' was having dinner last night at that Japanese restaurant where half the stuff was raw and all the other diners kept looking over at Sam while he pretended not to notice. Or breakfast this morning at that trendy café, where the omelette wasn't half as good as Mum's, all pale and tough like a kitchen sponge with bits of tomato inside, and where everyone looked at Sam once again and Sam sort of glowed with all the attention.

They were looking at him now, Luke realised, in that out-of-the-corner-of-their-eye way so it didn't seem like they were staring. Luke supposed Sam was used to it after so many years on TV. But it still made Luke feel weird.

'Attention! If the boys will all follow me ...' a teacher's voice said.

It's time, thought Luke. He looked up at Sam and tried to smile.

'You'll be right, mate,' said Sam confidently.

No way, thought Luke, as he followed the others in.

The hall was three times as large as the school hall at home, with big stained-glass windows at one end. The desks were polished wood. They looked as old and mellow as the school itself.

The teacher looked at his watch. 'Everyone got their pens? Right ... if anyone needs anything just raise your hand. You can start writing ... now!'

Luke lifted the exam paper and opened it. The maths section was first. The words blurred for a second, then cleared.

'If $3x = \ldots$' Luke stared. He felt a grin slide over his face. He knew this one! It had been on one of the old exam papers Sam had given him.

Maybe this wasn't going to be as bad as he'd thought.

He flicked over the other pages. 'Write an essay on one of the following ...' 'Examine the difference between State and Federal governments ...'

Cool! He knew it all! This was going to be easy ...

Too easy ... The thought went through him like an axe through butter.

How come he knew all the answers? He'd seen every question before, he'd answered them all before. He'd discussed and practised every essay ...

The paper on the desk in front of him looked just like the last exam paper he'd done back home, didn't it? The one Sam had insisted he complete totally, answering every question. 'Just to rehearse, you know.'

Luke tried to remember. It couldn't be just the same!

But it was.

There must have been a mix-up! They must have handed out last year's paper by mistake. He should put his hand up and tell them ...

Luke hesitated. Maybe they always repeated some of the questions each year. Or maybe ... maybe the mistake was the other way around. Maybe they'd sent him *this* year's exam instead of last year's.

Which meant he'd pass, he realised. It wouldn't be 'Dumb old Luke, pity he's not as bright as his stepdad.' He could really kill it ...

Luke picked up his pen. He was wasting time! He couldn't think about this now, he told himself. He'd do the exam, and then ... and then ...

And then there'd be time to work out what he should do ...

Chapter 2

Luke

Thunder. Enter the three Witches.
First Witch: Where hast thou been, Sister?
Second Witch: Killing swine.
(*Macbeth*, Act I, Scene 3, lines 1–2)

'The big question is,' said Mrs Easson, perching on the edge of her desk in front of the blackboard, 'what should Macbeth do? Should he believe the witches when they tell him he's going to be king?'

Luke yawned. How dumb was that? Witches. Who believed in witches these days?

Megan put up her hand. Luke grinned. This'd be good. Megan always had something to say.

'Witches are supposed to be wise women, aren't they? So Macbeth would be right to believe them.'

'Not in Shakespeare's time,' said Mrs Easson. 'Remember those were the days when women were hung for witchcraft. And James I, Shakespeare's king, hated witches. Which is probably why Shakespeare put them in his play — to make them so evil that the King would be pleased. Witches would have been a real crowd pleaser, too.'

'Shakespeare wanted to suck up to the King, then?' asked Megan.

'I wouldn't put it quite like that, but yes, to seek his favour,' said Mrs Easson. 'Shakespeare needed a licence from the King to put his plays on.'

'But that's what he was doing, wasn't he? Sucking up?' argued Megan.

Jingo put up his hand.

'Yes, James?' asked Mrs Easson, looking slightly startled. It was the first time Luke could remember Jingo putting up his hand in English. Showing off for Megan, thought Luke. He'd caught Jingo staring at Megan lately. He wondered if Megan had noticed.

'How come there aren't any vampires in *Macbeth*?'

Mrs Easson was taken aback. 'Why should there be?'

'Because they're heaps cooler than witches,' said Jingo. 'Vampires are hot!'

The class laughed.

Mrs Easson shook her head. 'English people didn't really think about vampires much till Bram Stoker wrote *Dracula*, in the late 1800s.' She grinned. 'Witches were the coolest topic around back then.' She looked around the class again. 'Any more questions before we move on?'

Jingo put up his hand again. 'How come Macbeth thought the women he met were witches? I mean, this guy's a real bright dude. How come he believes in witches?'

'Everybody did,' explained Mrs Easson. 'If someone thought you were a witch you were tortured till you confessed and then you were hanged.'

'Cool!' said someone.

Jingo's hand shot up again. 'What sort of tortures? I mean, did they pull out their fingernails . . .'

Mrs Easson's smile grew a bit more fixed. 'Maybe you'd like to look that up tonight then, James?'

'Sure. Can I change my talk to "Torturing Witches"?'

'No,' said Mrs Easson.

'Is this a thumbscrew that I see before me?' whispered Megan, not quite loudly enough for Mrs Easson to hear. A few people sniggered.

'But it doesn't make sense!' Jingo went on, glancing round to check that Megan was watching. 'There's this guy, right, and he's wandering through the fog and he meets these chicks. How come he suddenly thinks, Hey, yo, witches?'

'They had beards,' someone put in. 'Banquo says, "*you should be women, And yet your beards forbid me to interpret That you are so.*"'

'Good,' said Mrs Easson, impressed.

Megan put up her hand again. 'Women get hair on their faces after menopause, don't they?'

'Yeah,' put in Jingo. 'Mrs Henderson.'

Mrs Henderson was the principal. Luke joined in the general laughter.

'Now, now,' said Mrs Easson, though she was trying not to smile too.

'Hey, does that mean Mrs Henderson's a witch?' called Patrick.

More laughter.

'Settle down,' ordered Mrs Easson.

Jingo put his hand up again.

'What is it now, James?' she asked wearily.

'If I met Mrs Henderson in the fog,' said Jingo, 'and she told me I was going to be king one day, I wouldn't go and shoot what's his name, Prince Charles, like Macbeth goes and kills King Duncan. I'd just think she'd gone crazy.'

'Yay, King Jingo!' yelled someone up the back.

'But the witches were telling the truth,' objected Megan.

'Were they?' asked Mrs Easson. 'That's the point of the play, isn't it? Are they really telling Macbeth what *will* happen? Or are they lying to make Macbeth *try* to become king? Would he have become king if he'd never met them? Is it truth or is it a lie?'

Who cares? thought Luke. But it had been fun watching Megan take on Mrs Easson. Even Jingo had been okay.

He glanced at his watch. Nearly knock-off time. He supposed he'd better get round to reading the play tonight. Everyone else seemed to have finished it.

'Now, don't forget,' Mrs Easson said more loudly over the sound of the bell, 'you have to give your talks Friday of next week. Okay, off you go.'

Chairs scraped as the impatient ones who'd gathered up their things in the last five minutes of class raced for the door. Luke stood up more slowly. Why hurry? The bus never left till ten to four, which was when a couple of the kids on their route finished their music lessons.

'Hey, Luke.' It was Patrick. 'You finished reading the play yet?'

Pat and Megan lived next door, even if 'next door' meant five kilometres down the road — or one kilometre if you cut through the paddocks and went over the hill. Pat had been his best friend since they'd bashed each other with their rattles, and Megan, Pat's twin . . . well, she was just Megan. Part of Luke's life.

Luke shook his head. 'Haven't even started. How about you?'

'Nope. But Megan's read it.'

'Hey, not fair! You can't just have your sister read it instead of you.'

'Course I can,' said Patrick easily. 'One of the privileges of being a twin. Isn't that right, Meg?'

'What? No way!' Megan was shoving her books into her bag. 'You can read it yourself, peabrain.'

It was hard to believe that Megan and Pat were twins. Megan's hair was dark red — red like the rose on the bush Mum had planted in their new courtyard. Pat's was black, and he was a head taller than Megan too.

'Hey, Luke.' Megan turned to him. 'Dad wants to know if you can give us a hand pruning this weekend.' She wrinkled up her nose. 'I wish someone would come up with a peach tree that didn't need pruning . . .'

'Sure, no worries.' Luke liked pruning. Funny, he'd hated it when Dad was alive, when they *had* to prune the trees each winter or have no fruit to sell the next year. But since Sam had moved in and the orchards had been bulldozed, Luke had found he missed the trees and the old rhythm of their year.

At least he could still prune with Pat and Megan. And doing it with them was different somehow from pruning with your mum and dad.

The three of them walked along the splintery school verandah and down onto the asphalt. Luke could see the line of buses outside the school gates, the line of houses opposite, then behind them the paddocks and the bare brown hills. How many months since it's rained? he wondered. Three was it, or four?

'Hey, there's your mum!' said Megan. 'No, over there, dimwit, waving at you.'

'Mum? What's up?' For a moment Luke felt alarm. The last time Mum had come to school unexpectedly was the day that Dad died. She'd come from the hospital to pick Luke up and take him to Dad's bedside to say goodbye.

Dad had been breathing with that mask thing over his face, but when Luke bent down he'd breathed out, 'Look after your mum . . .'

It had been corny as hell, like Dad was copying the script out of some chicks' movie. Luke had been about to laugh, hoping Dad might smile as well, and then he'd seen Dad's eyes were staring at the ceiling and Mum . . .

'Luke!' Mum waved a letter in his face. She was wearing her old jeans with the rip in the knees, like she'd just rushed out without bothering to change into her go-to-town clothes, and her hair had a leaf in it. 'Stop dreaming! Look what came!'

'What is it?' asked Luke.

'Duh! It's a letter,' said Megan. 'Hey, it's addressed to you.'

'From St Ilf's,' said Mum. Her grin was so big it hardly fitted on her face. 'I opened it. I couldn't resist!'

'What's it say?'

'Don't you want to read it yourself?'

Luke shook his head. He'd failed . . . of course he'd failed . . .

... but Mum wouldn't be grinning like that if he'd failed.

Maybe they'd discovered the problem with the exam papers. Yeah, that'd be it. They would all have to do the exam again ...

'I'll read it if you're not going to!' said Megan impatiently.

Mum handed Megan the letter.

Mum was humming. She always did that when she was happy, even when someone else was talking. It used to drive Dad wild.

'Dear Luke, On behalf of the community of St Ilf's I have great pleasure in advising you ...' began Megan. Then she gasped. 'Luke!'

'What?' asked Luke nervously. 'Have they accepted me?'

'*Accepted* you? You peabrain! They've offered you a *scholarship*! You came top of the whole exam! Luke! I'm so happy for you!'

She was happy for him ... she was impressed. For a moment that was all Luke could take in.

And then the rest of it hit him. He'd won a scholarship! Dumb old Luke who'd nearly had to repeat Year Five, but that had been the year Dad died so they'd still let him go up a grade.

'Isn't it wonderful!' Mum did a little jig, clicking her fingers to the rhythm.

'Hey, Mum! Embarrassing!' hissed Luke.

'Sorry.' Mum didn't look sorry at all. But at least she stopped jigging.

'Hey, wait till Mrs Easson hears!' cried Patrick. 'And she only gave you sixty per cent last exam. That'll show her!'

'Sixty-three,' said Luke absently. He'd won a scholarship . . .

And then it hit him. He hadn't! That exam paper *had* been a mistake!

How had it happened? But that didn't matter now. He had to tell them . . . tell Mum . . .

'I rang Sam straightaway,' Mum was saying excitedly. 'He's flying back this afternoon. We'll pick him up on the way back home.'

Sam chartered a four-seater plane to take him to Sydney and back every week. Mum often went along too.

'What about his show?' asked Luke numbly.

'He's done a prerecord. They don't mind just this once, not with something like this. Oh, Luke, you've no idea how proud we are of you!'

'Me too,' said Megan. She sounded like she really meant it.

Usually she said 'us', Patrick and her together. But this was 'me', not 'us'.

He had to say something now!

But suddenly Mum was crying . . . It had been years since he'd seen Mum cry, not since the time after Dad died when the bank manager had driven out to tell her they couldn't keep on postponing the payments on the mortgage any more. They'd have to sell the farm . . . Then a week later she'd met Sam at the reunion and it had all been okay. But that night she'd cried and cried as though she'd never stop. He'd wanted to help her, but he hadn't known how . . .

Now she was crying again, but they were tears of joy. 'You'll never know what this means to me, Luke. I was so worried . . . you'd missed so much school when your dad was sick. I thought it was all my fault, that I should have helped you more. But you've made it all up, and more!'

'Mum, it was never your fault ...' began Luke, then stopped. This wasn't the place to say all that. People were staring at them already.

'Hey, are you lot getting on the bus or what?' yelled Jingo to Megan and Pat.

'I can give you a lift ...' Mum began, but Megan was already waving the letter in the air.

'Guess what?' she yelled to Jingo. 'Luke's won a scholarship!'

Too late, thought Luke. There was no way now he could say anything at all.

Chapter 3

Luke

... a tale
Told by an idiot, full of sound and fury,
Signifying nothing.

(*Macbeth*, Act V, Scene 5, lines 26–28)

Luke shoved his copy of *Macbeth* to the back of his desk. What did all those old words mean, anyway? he thought as he opened the window. His bedroom stank of air freshener. It always had that not-quite-roses smell after Mrs Tomlin cleaned.

Mrs Tomlin and her husband lived in the cottage down past the machinery shed. The cottage had just been a wreck when Mum and Dad had the farm. But when Sam married Mum he'd had the cottage renovated at the same time as the new wing of the house was built.

Now Mrs Tomlin did the housework, and the cooking too when Mum went down to stay with Sam during the week in Sydney, and Mr Tomlin helped Mum run the farm. Mum and Sam slept in the new part of the house, but Luke had kept his old bedroom.

He breathed in the night air gratefully. Cold cowpat wasn't the best smell in the world. But at least it was a real smell. Better than air freshener.

It was three days now since the letter had come from St Ilf's. Three days of people congratulating him, telling him 'Well done.' Three days of empty triumph. Mum had been walking around with a grin the entire time, singing 'Rocky Mountain High' under her breath. You always knew Mum was over the moon when she sang 'Rocky Mountain High'.

How could he ever tell Mum he'd cheated?

But he hadn't really cheated, he told himself. Cheating was when you meant to do it. How was he to know that the exam paper would be one he'd seen before?

If only he hadn't won a scholarship! If he'd just passed the entrance exam it wouldn't have been so bad. It wasn't even as though he needed it. Sam had plenty of money. And now everyone would expect this brilliant kid and instead they'd just get dumb old Luke. He didn't even want to go to school in Sydney, away from all his friends.

If only he'd mentioned that he'd already seen the exam paper immediately ... or at least when the letter came. But if he said anything now everyone would think he *had* cheated. And it'd break Mum's heart.

'Look after your mum,' Dad had said. Looking after Mum back then had meant keeping the wood box full of kindling and making her a cup of tea when she came in from the paddocks. Not this ...

Luke sighed and looked at the book again. He couldn't concentrate on *Macbeth* now. Maybe over the weekend ... There was still all of next week anyway before his talk was due. Mrs Easson had treated him differently since she'd learned about the scholarship, as though she really listened to what he said now. She'd probably expect a brilliant talk, too.

Luke undressed slowly. There was no one to say goodnight to tonight; Sam and Mum weren't due back till tomorrow. Mum had flown back to Sydney with Sam after the scholarship celebrations. Mrs Tomlin had left dinner for Luke in the oven. Tuna Surprise — though the only surprise Luke could see was that no one dropped dead after eating it. He wished Mrs Tomlin would stop thinking she could cook, and give him a frozen pizza instead.

The sheets were cold. Central heating never seemed to warm sheets, not like the true heat of summer. Of course the house was air conditioned too now, but he could still remember the summer when Dad had died, the way the bed still seemed to sweat no matter how late Luke went to sleep. And that winter when the toilet froze and the pipes cracked and Mum went frantic because she couldn't pay a plumber ...

Luke shut his eyes. Mum hated him talking about those days. She wanted 'now' to be the only world there was ... the 'everything is perfect' life, with a TV-star husband and a son who'd won a scholarship.

What should he do?

At least in Shakespeare's world things were clear, thought Luke, almost asleep. You knew what was right and wrong in those days ... If only I lived in a world like that ...

Macbeth's world, with its swords and witches ...

Witches ...

Chapter 4

Lulach

The Weïrd Sisters, hand in hand . . .
(*Macbeth*, Act I, Scene 3, line 32)

The three witches were stirring the cauldron that hung in the big fireplace at the end of the great Hall.

Lulach stood on tiptoe to peer inside. 'What's in the pot today?'

Six months had passed, autumn and winter, since his father's death. Food had been short. Many in Alba were close to starvation — or worse. All there'd been to eat yesterday was seaweed stew, with a few shellfish in it that the women had gathered along the shore. No barley to thicken it, no oatcakes baking on the hearth. No meat either, and the best of the spring milk kept for the calves . . .

It had been a desperate winter. Even Lulach had to admit that the new Mormaer had done his best. But with the men away so much last summer the barley harvest had been poor, and there hadn't been enough fish dried either. And since King Duncan lost the last war, Thorfinn had been sending his men raiding along the coast.

The Norse ships were fast and narrow, like spears bringing horror and death. They left the land empty: crops burned, the dead lying where they'd fallen, while the living, men, women and children, were herded into Norse ships to be sold at the Dublin slave markets.

Thorfinn's men hadn't come to Moray yet. But Lulach had heard of a fishing village further north where all the survivors of Thorfinn's raid had jumped over the cliffs onto the rocks below, sons carrying their old parents, mothers with their children in their arms. A swift death on the rocks was better than a slow death by starvation.

Lulach's tummy rumbled. Something smelled good today. Better than seaweed stew.

Meröe grinned, showing her hard red gums, and gave the cauldron a stir. 'Fillet of a fenny snake,' she whispered, the hairs on her chin quivering like a billy goat's. 'Eye of newt and toe of frog . . .'

'No,' insisted Lulach, 'what's really in there?'

Meröe laughed and ruffled his hair. Lulach wished she wouldn't do that.

'Venison. His Lordship had a good hunt last night. And kale and nettles to make you strong.'

Lulach said nothing. The new Mormaer had hardly spoken to him since he'd been elected last summer. He had more to occupy him than one small boy, though he'd been friendly enough.

But Lulach hated him. This was the man who'd taken his father's place. Even his hair was wrong: red instead of yellow like his father's.

But Lulach said nothing. What was there to say? The people had voted for the new Mormaer. The land needed a leader.

Lulach took the big horn spoon from beside the pot and scooped out a spoonful of meat then blew on it to cool it down.

His mother had told him that when the mormaers met at Scone to elect a king, people ate from big trenchers of soft white wheat bread, two people sharing the same trencher. Lulach had never tasted wheat bread, and here in the north everyone at the rath ate out of the one big pot. Even the people who slept in their own cottages came up to the Hall to eat.

The venison stew tasted good. Better than barley porridge or dried fish. *Much* better than seaweed stew. When I'm a man, thought Lulach, I'll hunt every day. No one will ever have to eat seaweed stew again.

Clang! Clang!

It was the sound of a sword beating on a shield. The danger call!

Lulach dropped the spoon. The stew splashed on his stockings, but he took no notice.

A woman screamed. Someone in the courtyard yelled, 'Smoke! Smoke from the watch fires on the cliff!' And then the terrible word: 'Norsemen!'

Thorfinn's men! thought Lulach. The black skull flashed before his eyes again. Thorfinn, the man he had to kill one day ...

'Grab what you can!' a woman cried. 'They won't find us in the hills!'

Someone began to sob.

'Stop snivelling!' The Lady Gruoch strode into the Hall, still wearing the long white apron that she put on when checking the cheeses. 'Do you think our Mormaer will let Norsemen reach the Hall? Ealdith, send a runner down to the bull yards to tell him —'

Hoof beats clattered on the cobbles out in the courtyard. 'Sounds like his Lordship knows already,' muttered Meröe.

Lulach ran outside.

His stepfather sat tall and straight on his brown horse, his thick red plaits touching his shoulders. Behind him Kenneth grabbed the reins of another horse from the blacksmith. 'Will I send out the runners to fetch the men from the far fields, my Lord?'

'No time,' said the Mormaer shortly. 'They'll have the crops burned and every child along the coast trussed up in slave ropes before the runners can deliver their messages. Who's here at the Hall?'

Kenneth counted on his fingers. 'Girc Blacksmith, Bodhe One Eye, Dugald and Angus the bowmen ... and you and I, my Lord.'

The big man laughed. 'Six of us, eh? It'll have to do!'

Kenneth stared. 'But, my Lord, the lookout says six ships! That's more than a hundred men!'

'Then we'll use brains instead of swords. Tell Angus to bring his arrows. My Lady,' to Lulach's mother, 'I need oil and rags. Linen, not wool or hide.'

How can you fight Norsemen with oil and rags? wondered Lulach. They needed men with swords! This man was a fool! But Lulach's mother nodded and slipped back into the Hall.

Kenneth too stared at his new chief as though he were crazy. 'My Lord, there's no way six men can stop a Norse raid! We need to wait till the fishers see the watch smoke and bring their boats in.'

The new mormaer stared at him. 'And have a proper battle, eh? Like one of Duncan's? Men slashing at each other till enough have been killed or crippled, and the raiders go away?'

Kenneth shook his head, puzzled. 'What else can we do, my Lord? We have to wait till we have enough men —'

'Who is mormaer here? You or me?'

'You, my Lord, but —'

'I will not start my time as chief by losing half my men! Now, are you coming with me or not?'

'Of course, my Lord, but —'

'Move!' roared the Mormaer. His horse tossed its head and danced across the cobbles at the noise.

It was like a spring wind melting the ice. Women ran, their terror vanished, at least for now, bringing horses, rags. Girc and Bodhe hastily strapped on their swords. Lulach's mother ran out of the Hall again, with a jar of precious oil.

The Mormaer bent down from his horse to take the oil. Lulach stiffened as the Mormaer kissed his wife, then stuffed the rags into the belt of his smock.

It still hurt Lulach whenever he saw the Mormaer kiss his mother. It hurt to see him take charge like this too.

It should be his father there. Or him . . .

Maybe the Norsemen would kill his stepfather too. Lulach felt a stab of guilty pleasure at the thought.

But if they killed the Mormaer they'd burn the crops before the harvest. They'd round up Moray's people for their slave ships . . .

Duty, thought Lulach. A chief has a duty to his people. And I'm a chief's son, even if he's dead.

'My Lord!' Lulach found his voice. He ran up to the big horse. 'Take me as well!'

'Lulach . . .'

Lulach heard Kenneth laugh and a ripple of amusement from the watching women. 'I can fight the Norsemen!' he cried indignantly.

His stepfather didn't laugh. He didn't even smile. He bent down from the saddle again and touched Lulach's shoulder briefly with his free hand. 'When you can lift a sword you can come with me. But for now, look after your mother and the Hall.'

'I can so lift a sword!' cried Lulach. 'Kenneth has been teaching me and Knut with wooden swords for ages . . . since St Andrew's Day!'

'All of six months, eh?' said the Mormaer admiringly, but now there was laughter in his voice. 'I'm sorry, lad, but —'

'One day I might be mormaer! It's my duty to go!'

'Lulach!' said his mother. 'This isn't the time —'

But the Mormaer held up his hand. He looked down at Lulach consideringly. Almost, thought Lulach, as though his stepfather had never really looked at him before. 'Mormaer of Moray? Well, so you may be . . .' A strong hand reached down. 'Climb up then, my son!'

It was the first time his stepfather had called him 'son'.

It was strange to be sitting so high up again. He hadn't been up on a big horse since his father had ridden away. Lulach felt he could see the whole world — the green hills and the mist, the river then the dark waters of the firth beyond the Hall.

But below him people muttered.

'A child! He's taking a child!'

'The boy will be killed!'

'And if he's killed, whose son will be Mormaer of Moray next?' It was Meröe's voice.

Lulach heard his mother say, 'Meröe! Inside! Now!'

But his stepfather only smiled. He reached down a hand to his wife and touched her hair. They were large hands, callused across the palm from wielding a sword. Father's hands were like that, thought Lulach. One day my hands will be like that too.

'I'll look after him,' the Mormaer said softly, one hand holding Lulach and the reins as well. 'Trust me.'

Lulach's mother nodded, her plaits bouncing under her yellow scarf, which marked her out as a married woman. 'I do.'

Then they were off.

Out of the courtyard, over the cobbles, then on to the muddy track and past the outlying cottages, each with their patch of green crinkled kale. If only Knut could see me, though Lulach. But Knut was with the cattle up on the hills.

It never occurred to Lulach that perhaps this would be the day he'd die. Death was for grown-ups. Not for him.

Suddenly the Mormaer pulled at the reins. The horse veered away from the track that led down to the beach, then galloped across the heather. The other horses followed. Birds burst in fright out of the bushes then flapped away.

'My Lord!' Lulach had to yell above the sound of hoof beats.

'Yes?'

'We're going the wrong way! The Norsemen are on the shore! Down that way!'

He felt as much as heard the rumble of his stepfather's laugh again. 'I know where the beach is by now! But if we gallop along the shore they'll see us.'

'Shouldn't we have brought the dogs?'

Another rumble. 'We're not hunting today!' Then more seriously, 'Well, perhaps we are. Lulach, will you do as I tell you? Without question?'

Lulach considered. 'Yes,' he yelled at last, as the horse jumped over a larger puddle than before.

'Why?'

'Because . . . because you're my stepfather?'

'No. Because I'm the leader and this is a party of war. And if I'm killed, then Kenneth is the leader, and you obey him. That's the way war has to be. No arguing. No questions. A question might kill us all. You understand?'

'Yes,' said Lulach unwillingly.

'Good,' said his stepfather softly. 'A tanist needs to learn when to be quiet as well as when to question.'

Lulach felt his heart lurch. Was the Mormaer really going to make him his heir? But the big man said nothing more. They galloped on.

They could see the sea again now, grey water under the grey sky — like dog fur almost, thought Lulach. His father had called fish 'the silver harvest', so much easier to gather than the golden grain, which had to be coaxed from the soil.

Suddenly Lulach saw something else: a flash of red and brown lying by the track. They cantered closer, and Lulach saw it was a body. The man must have been running to the Hall when the Norsemen caught him and sliced through his neck with their swords. His head had rolled into the heather. One hand was missing too. He must have worn a ring, thought Lulach. It was too tight to pull off, so the Norsemen cut off his hand to get it.

He thought, I won't be sick. I won't.

They were close to the sea now. Suddenly white smoke floated up above the hills. The smoke turned black. Then there was more of it, and more . . .

'They're burning the barley,' muttered the Mormaer.

Lulach knew what that meant. Another winter of hunger, especially if the raiders reached the main fields around the Hall. And what if they reached the Hall itself?

The Mormaer turned his horse to face the other riders. 'The ships are around the bay,' he said softly. 'No talking now. Follow my lead.'

There was a sheep path that led down to the water. Lulach had been that way before, gathering seaweed with the women. How had a stranger like his stepfather known of it?

A hare peered up at them from the heather, all long ears and startled gaze, then darted into cover. The Mormaer held up his hand again. They dismounted and tethered the horses to a stunted tree.

'My Lord!' Kenneth spoke in a harsh whisper.

'Yes?'

'Leave the boy here!'

'No!' cried Lulach, just as his stepfather said, 'As he said, it's his duty. Do you deny him that?'

37

'No. But —'

'He'll be safer with us,' said the Mormaer shortly. He thrust the pot of oil at Lulach. 'Look after it,' he said softly.

'Yes, my Lord,' whispered Lulach.

They crept along the shingle of the beach. The wind spat in their faces and ruffled the waves. Lulach's leather shoes crunched on the pebbles, so loudly that he was sure the Norsemen would hear him. He wished he had bare feet, like Angus and Dugald.

What if the Norsemen did hear them?

I'll slow the others down if we have to run away, thought Lulach. Or would his stepfather leave him behind if they had to run? It wouldn't be fair for the others to die because of his short legs.

For the first time he wondered if he'd done the right thing.

The Mormaer pointed to a clump of trees with twisted trunks. The men and the boy slipped behind them. Lulach peered through the branches.

The Norse ships bobbed on the waves: long swift raiders, each with a single man guarding it. Their ship's boats were pulled up onto the shore.

'See the sail?' whispered the Mormaer. 'That's Thorfinn's sign.'

Thorfinn! Lulach hadn't thought his heart could pound so hard. 'Where is he?' he whispered fiercely.

The Mormaer glanced down at him. 'Shh, lad! He won't have come himself. Dugald, Angus, can your arrows reach the ships?'

Angus hesitated. 'The nearest ship, perhaps,' he said. 'But I couldn't hit a man from here!'

'Just hit the ship — the deck if you can, not the sail or sides. Think you can do that?'

Angus nodded.

'Good lad. Dugald, can you get to the other side of the cove without them seeing you?'

'Aye, my Lord. Over the hill, then behind those rocks . . .'

'Do it. When you see your brother's arrow, you fire too. Now, pass me one of your arrows.'

What use is a single arrow? thought Lulach, as the young man handed it over.

The Mormaer tied rags around the arrow head. 'Lulach, the oil!' he whispered.

Lulach handed him the oil. His stepfather poured it onto the rags till they were soaked, then pulled a tinderbox from his pouch. He opened the box and picked out some rotten wood and dried fungus, then struck at the flint with the steel. A spark flashed then went out.

The Mormaer struck again. The tinder flared. The Mormaer held the oil-soaked rags against the flames.

Long seconds passed. Nothing happened. Then the rags began to smoulder. Lulach held his breath. Would the Norsemen see the smoke?

The rags burst into flame. Suddenly the smoke was clear, shimmering around the burning arrow.

Kenneth's expression changed. 'I see,' he said softly. 'This might just work.'

'It *will* work.' The Mormaer handed Dugald the burning arrow. 'Now run, lad! Run!'

Dugald ran, the flaming arrow in his hand. The Mormaer handed another burning arrow to Angus.

The smoke made Lulach cough. He bit his lip to silence it.

'Good lad,' whispered the Mormaer. He stared out at the bobbing ships. 'Now!' he ordered Angus.

The arrow flew. Its flames flared, then disappeared.

Thunk! Someone yelled from the one of the ships as the arrow plunged down onto the deck.

Nothing happened.

'The flame went out!' Lulach whispered in dismay.

'Shh,' returned his stepfather. 'It's smouldering. Watch.'

A wisp of smoke, almost too faint to see. Then black smoke, then more ... and suddenly the deck was burning. The man on board shouted and grabbed a cloak to beat at the flames.

A bird flew across the cove ... but it wasn't a bird, Lulach realised. It was Dugald's arrow, flaming across the sky.

Thunk! The arrow hit the furthest boat. More yells from on board, and from down in the cove.

'Burn, you Norse scum, burn!' muttered Kenneth.

Lulach glanced at him, shocked at the hatred in his voice.

'I heard your father's death screams,' explained Kenneth softly. 'Fifty men trapped in a wooden fort. Let the Norsemen feel the kiss of fire now.'

The first ship was burning fiercely now, its guard trying frantically to scoop up water and put it out.

Lulach shivered. What would happen to the guard on the ship? he wondered suddenly. Would he become burned and twisted too?

He wanted to yell to the guard to jump away from the flames. But the guard was a Norseman, an enemy. He was one of Thorfinn's men! He deserved to die!

And anyway, if Lulach yelled, the enemy would find them all and they'd die too . . .

The guard gave a shriek and dived over the side. For a moment Lulach thought he had drowned. Then his head appeared, and his hands, holding an oar to keep himself afloat.

The flames had begun to eat up the second ship as well. Smoke billowed up into the sky.

'I could get an arrow into another ship if I ran down to the shore,' offered Angus.

The Mormaer shook his head. 'Nay, lad, they'd kill you for it. They have four ships left. Better they sail away in those than we have a mob of shipless Norsemen stranded on our beaches.'

Suddenly Norsemen spilled down the track to the beach, wearing round metal helmets, with axes, swords or burning torches in their hands. They milled around, yelling, wondering where the enemy lay.

'One more arrow,' said the Mormaer quietly. 'Not a burning one this time. Angus, can you hit the redhead with the jewelled sword? He seems to be the leader.'

'Aye, my Lord. I think so.'

'Do it.'

Thwak! Suddenly the man crumpled, bright blood spilling from the arrow in his neck.

'Good shot,' said the Mormaer calmly.

'Our father taught us well,' said Angus.

So did mine, thought Lulach. He was beginning to wonder if this new stepfather might not have lessons for him too.

Thwak! Another arrow hissed from Dugald's end of the cove. A second Viking fell, clutching at the arrow through his eye.

The Norsemen on the beach seemed to be arguing. Some pointed to the burning ships, others to the hills behind.

Lulach held his breath. The Vikings would soon find them if they began to hunt. Or could they run away in time?

But warriors didn't run. Or did they? There was more to the art of warfare, he realised, than holding a broadsword.

Suddenly the Norsemen seemed to come to a decision. Men rushed for the small boats pulled up high on the beach. Hands grabbed oars as they rowed back to the remaining ships. Sails rose towards the sky.

'They can't tell how many of us are hidden,' said the Mormaer with satisfaction. 'And if just one more boat burns there won't be room for them all.'

'My Lord, four more flaming arrows and we could burn the lot of them!' urged Kenneth.

The Mormaer shook his head. 'Two lost ships will teach Thorfinn not to attack Moray lands again in a hurry. Six lost ships calls for revenge. No, let them go.'

'But, my Lord —'

'I've spoken,' said the Mormaer.

This time Kenneth gave in without further argument. They watched as, one by one, the rowers grabbed the oars, the sails rose and the Norse ships headed back towards the sea.

'Well done, men,' said the Mormaer, speaking normally now.

He sounds like it was nothing, thought Lulach wonderingly. As though six men and a boy beat an invading army every day.

'Kenneth, order a watch be kept along the cliffs, in case they change their minds.' The Mormaer smiled down at Lulach. 'Well, my son? What did you think of your first battle?'

Lulach shook his head in confusion. What had he felt? He didn't know. Triumph, terror, pity, hatred, horror, joy ... no words could describe it. And the Mormaer had called him 'son' for the second time that day.

Is that how he thinks of me? Lulach wondered. Am I really a son to him?

This stepfather was looking at him thoughtfully. And then he smiled. 'Yes,' he said at last. 'You'll make a good tanist, lad. The best that I could have.'

They cantered back across the fields. Men ran to meet them, armed with hoes and pitchforks, or hastily grabbed swords. Women stared at them, clutching children on their hips and bundles on their backs, ready to run to the hills.

But there was no need to run now.

The cheers began as Kenneth yelled the news. Women waved their scarves in the air, men brandished pitchforks. The Mormaer waved. He looked ... sort of bigger, Lulach thought. As though the love and admiration were food like bread and cheese.

'They'll sing of you for a thousand years, my Lord!' Kenneth shouted above the noise.

A thousand years, thought Lulach. Will our names still be known a thousand years from now?

In front of him his stepfather smelled of smoke and sweat and horse and something else as well.

Glory, thought Lulach, as they rode into the courtyard and his mother's hands helped him down. I know what glory smells like now.

This is what it's like, he thought, to have a hero as a stepfather.

Chapter 5

Luke

Lady Macduff: Sirrah, your father's dead:
    And what will you do now? How will you live?
Son: As birds do, mother.
Lady Macduff: What, with worms and flies?
           (*Macbeth*, Act IV, Scene 2, lines 30–32)

That's what it would be like to have a hero as a stepfather, thought Luke, lying back in bed and staring at the faint light of morning out the window. A real hero, not just one who knew how to make himself look good on TV.

Lulach was a hero too, Luke thought. Not a coward like me.

But it would have been easy to be a hero in those days. You knew who the enemy was, knew what you had to do.

It had been the best dream . . .

Maybe if he went back to sleep he could go back to it. Today was Saturday, there was no need to get up for school.

He shut his eyes again. But it was no use.

He got out of bed slowly and began to pull on his jeans. Already the TV was muttering in the kitchen, where Mrs T was making breakfast. Sam's show, *Wake Up Call*, started at eight o'clock, though Saturday's program was just the repeated highlights of the week's news. But Mrs T never missed an episode.

Luke hoped Mrs T wasn't making her corn fritters, with the blob of chutney in the middle like something out of a baby's nappy. Or the tomatoes stuffed with puke. Mrs T seemed to have spent her life cutting recipes out of magazines, and every one of them involved something stuffed with something else. Luke bet Mrs T's idea of heaven was being able to find something to stuff into a boiled egg.

What would Lulach have eaten for breakfast? Duh! thought Luke. I'm acting like the dream was real. Real was never as good as that.

Yeah, the people had been hungry — Luke had felt his guts heave at the idea of seaweed stew — and most of the men in the fields had been barefoot despite the chill in the air. But they'd been proud too. No one had been pretending in that world ... like Luke pretending to have won that scholarship, like Sam on TV pretending to care about the planet ...

Luke wondered what Sam would be yakking on about today. Baby seals in Canada, maybe, being slaughtered for fur coats. Something that would make people go 'How terrible' while they ate their toast, so they could feel like good concerned citizens.

Luke thought of the Mormaer in his dream. He didn't talk about things. He did them. A fighter ...

Luke had never had a dream like that before. Mostly dreams started out okay and then got muddled. But that dream had been like ... like something on TV. No, not like TV. You couldn't feel TV. But he'd felt the warmth of the horse on his legs, the calluses of the Mormaer's hands. He'd tasted the venison and kale.

The dream had been *real*.

Luke snorted. How soft could he get? Real dreams? No way. He'd been reading *Macbeth* before he went to sleep, that was all. So he'd dreamed of swords and witches and bad guys like ... what was the Norseman in his dream? Thorfinn ... a villain, like Macbeth ...

And heroes like Macduff or the Mormaer, and a time when things were simple ... you fought the invaders, you were loyal to your friends. There was no need to lie or cheat ...

Luke ran a comb through his hair and headed out to the kitchen.

Mrs T was turning something in the frying pan. Luke felt his stomach clench. But he didn't want to offend her by refusing it. He wondered what they had for breakfast at St Ilf's. It couldn't be any worse than what Mrs T served up.

Mrs T slid a plate of pancakes in front of him.

'Thanks,' he muttered.

'Lemon juice or maple syrup?' she asked.

'Syrup, thanks.' It wasn't real maple syrup. Maple syrup came from trees; he'd done a project on them in Year Three, the year that Dad got sick. This was artificial stuff. But he supposed it tasted much the same.

He took a bite of pancake. Yuck — what *were* those things? For a moment he thought they might be rabbit droppings. But then he realised they were blueberries.

He took another bite. The blueberries were tasteless and the pancakes were burned on the bottom, but for once they weren't that bad.

Luke glanced up at the TV on the bench. There was Sam's face, with its concerned look and orange make-up.

'And so we're left with one question,' he was saying. 'Is the Japanese Government sincere when it says the Japanese need to kill whales for scientific purposes? And if it's lying — why? Coming up next: a terrorist or hero? You decide.'

Mrs T ran the sponge over the bench. 'He really knows how to say things, doesn't he?'

'Yeah,' said Luke shortly. He wondered what Mrs T would say if she knew other people researched Sam's scripts, and even wrote them for him.

'What are you up to today?'

Luke shrugged. 'Going over to the Fishers'.'

'Don't be late for dinner. Your mum said they'd fly in this morning.'

'I won't be.' Luke pushed the plate away.

'Are you sure you wouldn't like another . . .' began Mrs T.

'No, really, that was great, thanks,' said Luke hurriedly. He grabbed his jacket from the hook by the door and galloped outside before she could even think of muffins with mashed banana inside, or her special 'health' mixture of orange juice, oatbran and milk.

The world smelled different out of doors. Cold gum leaves, colder soil ... Luke bet he could tell what season it was even with his eyes shut. Even barbed wire smelled different in winter, when it was hung with frozen spiders' webs and frost.

He crossed the gravel courtyard and passed the garage — only the ute and Mr T's car in there today; Mum had left the four-wheel drive at the airport.

Home looked so different these days. The old weatherboard house that his great-grandparents had built was hidden behind the new verandah and dwarfed by the brick extensions. Even the fences were new.

Luke opened the gate to the house paddock and poked one of the cowpats with his toe. Cowpats were different in winter too, with white frost whiskers and a pond of dew in the middle. In summer they got a crust almost as soon as they'd plopped out, and then the dung beetles got to them.

The cows gazed at him hopefully, then bent their heads again. They were Simmentals, about two months from calving, with soft caramel-brown coats and even browner eyes.

Mum loved cows. She'd started with three of them, when she and Dad took over the three hundred hectares of run-down orchard and scrub from Pop and Nanna, before Luke was born. They'd been Herefords in those days.

The Simmentals were Sam's idea. More money per unit in good stock, he'd said. Luke bet that Sam liked being able to call the place a stud, not just a farm. But Luke liked the Simmentals too. They were a restful sort of cow, as though they were sure the world would always be full of lush grass, or at least good hay.

The old orchards were under irrigated lucerne these days, and the paddocks green even in winter from improved pasture and superphosphate. But it'd be good to have more land too, thought Luke.

Sometimes he dreamed about buying a place of his own when he left school. Raising Japanese Wagyu cattle, maybe. There looked to be real opportunities with Wagyu. But land cost so much these days. He'd seen what struggling under a big mortgage had done to Mum and Dad.

The cows had given up hoping he'd brought them some hay and gone back to munching grass. Luke ducked through the barbed-wire fence onto the Fishers' land and started up the hill. No improved pasture here, just tufts of native grass under the wattle trees, pittosporums in the gullies, then gums as he climbed higher. Sam said they were 'Eucalyptus smithii', but Dad had called them 'gully gums' — not much use for fence posts, with too much ash for firewood but good for a chook house in a pinch.

Would there be anywhere to walk like this at St Ilf's? The grounds looked so small and neat. It'd be weird to have to live with strangers, in a strange country, where everything you saw belonged to someone else ... But he wasn't going to think about that today.

He was at the top of the hill now. He and Pat and Meg used to play Explorers up here when they were little, pretending no one had ever been this way before — carefully ignoring the cows and the fences, the thin line of the beach twenty ks away, with the smudge of town buildings beside it.

He could see the Fishers' house from here too, with its haze of smoke above the chimney, packing shed, hay shed, tractor and the orchards straggling down to the creek and part way up the next hill. There were three figures in the far orchard, underneath the leafless peach trees. Patrick and Megan and their dad, pruning.

'Hoy!'

The distant figures looked up. One waved. Luke grinned and jogged down the hill towards them.

Chapter 6

Luke

When the hurlyburly's done ...
(*Macbeth*, Act I, Scene 1, line 3)

It was good spending a few hours pruning. Doing real work, not like most of what he did at school. It was something he really missed at home now. Of course, it was great that Mum had Mr T to do all the hard work these days. But it meant that she didn't really need Luke's help at all.

It was different at the Fishers'. The Fishers took it for granted he'd help with whatever was going on. Just like they'd helped him and Mum after Dad died.

Snip, snip ... It took years to learn to prune a peach tree properly. If you didn't prune off enough the fruit would be too small to sell, and there wouldn't be much fruit next year either. But if you cut too much away there'd be no fruit at all. *Snip, snip* ...

Luke glanced over at the others. Mr Fisher worked like a machine, *snip, snip, snip*, and Patrick looked just like him only younger. But Megan kept staring into the distance like she wasn't thinking of peach trees at all.

Luke grinned to himself. Knowing Meg she was probably miles away. Maybe reliving the last book she'd read ... He liked the way her hair still hung down her back in that ponytail. When he was small he used to pull it. He wished he still could ...

The sun was high above the valley by the time they'd finished the orchard. Mr Fisher shoved the secateurs into the pouch at his belt. 'Well, that's that done,' he said, nodding a thanks to Luke. 'See you up at the house, kids.'

The tractor muttered behind them as he took the prunings off to be burned.

'Hey, did you finish reading *Macbeth*?' Megan asked Luke as they all walked up the road to the house.

'Nope,' said Luke.

'Me neither,' said Patrick. 'You're going to have to help me with my talk, Meg,' he added.

Megan fished a bit of peach bark out of her hair and threw it at him. 'No way!'

'Swap you the washing up for a week.'

Megan considered. 'Well, maybe ...'

'What did Mrs Easson say you had to give your talk on?' asked Luke.

'"*Macbeth*'s Comic Elements",' said Patrick gloomily, kicking a rock off the road. 'What comic elements? There's nothing funny about *Macbeth*.'

'The porter,' suggested Megan. 'He's drunk.'

'Drunk's not enough to be funny,' said Patrick. 'I mean, everyone isn't outside the pub every Saturday night going "Ha, ha, ha, look at them all", are they?'

'They probably didn't have much to laugh about back in Shakespeare's time,' said Megan. 'I mean, like

53

no TV or anything, just a play or a dancing bear if you were lucky. All those diseases, and most of your kids dying.'

'How do you know all that stuff?' asked Luke.

''Cause she's a nerd,' said Patrick, even more gloomily. 'Now my best mate's won a scholarship and he's turning into a nerd too. I'm surrounded by nerds. Meg'll be doing crosswords at lunch next.'

'Nah. Just a few maths problems before I go to bed. They're, like, so relaxing — hey, joke!' Megan added, when Luke stared at her. 'What's your topic?'

'"Macbeth's Slide into Villainy",' quoted Luke. 'I've got to show how Macbeth's just an okay guy at first, then the witches tell him he'll be king and he gets ambitious and kills everyone off and goes mad.'

'Jingo had the right idea,' said Patrick enviously. 'His brother was in Mrs Easson's class last year so he knew what to expect. He asked if he could do Macbeth's weapons. You know, swords and stuff.'

'Cool,' said Luke.

'You should have chosen Shakespeare's rude words,' said Megan helpfully.

'Rude words?'

'Yeah. Like, all sorts of words in Shakespeare's plays were really rude back then. But their meanings have changed so we don't realise how rude they were. Like "will".'

'What did "will" mean?' asked Luke curiously.

Megan blushed. 'Er, can't remember ... Hey, Mum's back from town,' she added, noticing the car out the front of the house.

The kitchen was stuffy from the big fuel stove and too hot after the work outside. Mrs Fisher was unpacking groceries on the old blue-painted table. 'Hi, Luke,' she said. 'Megan, open a couple of cans of soup, will you? You must all be starved. Pat, stick some wood on the fire. George,' as Mr Fisher came in behind them, 'mail's on the table.'

Luke began to set the table. He knew the Fishers' kitchen as well as his own. Better, probably, because it was Mrs T's kitchen these days as much as it was Mum's. Mum liked cooking, as long as Mrs T did the washing up. They never had canned soup these days at home. He supposed Mum had more time to cook than Mrs Fisher.

Mr Fisher plonked himself down on a kitchen chair and began to open the letters. 'Postcard from Auntie Ted,' he said. Then he frowned. 'What's this from the Council?' He opened it and began to read.

Suddenly he stiffened. 'Holy hell!' he muttered.

Megan stared at him, the soup forgotten. 'Dad, what's wrong?'

Mr Fisher shook his head. He handed the letter to his wife. It was only a paragraph, Luke noticed. What could be so bad in a paragraph?

'Mum? What's going on?' demanded Megan.

Mrs Fisher passed the letter to Megan. 'They're going to build a resort up on Paterson's old place,' she said dazedly.

'A resort!' Patrick said the word like he'd never heard it before.

'But that's next door!' said Luke. 'Why on earth would they want to build there?'

'Why not?' Megan looked up from the letter. 'It's got the river, and the view's incredible, right down the valley. You can even glimpse the sea up there. It says there's going to be a golf course and everything . . .'

'Water,' said Mr Fisher flatly.

'What?'

'Golf courses need water. All that grass. More water even than orchards. Then there's water for the swimming pool . . .'

'Spas,' said Mrs Fisher helplessly. 'Those places have those spa baths, don't they?'

'But they can't!' cried Patrick. 'That's our water!'

'Not till it gets here, it isn't,' said Mr Fisher. He looked stunned, as though someone had hit him on the head. 'We only just scraped through with enough water last summer. This is going to ruin us. The Stevensons too, maybe.' The Stevensons farmed further downstream.

'What about the animals?' said Megan. 'The platypuses in the creek?'

'Platypuses?' said Patrick scornfully.

'Well, they have a right to be here too!' returned Megan. 'And what's the town going to be like with all those tourists? And the road . . . it's not made for lots of cars. And —'

'Who cares?' Patrick cut in. 'Roads, platypuses . . . it's going to destroy our farm. You can't grow fruit without water. *That's* what matters.'

'But . . . but they can't just do something like that, can they?' asked Luke. 'Just move in and take your water?' He felt stunned.

Megan thrust the letter back at her mother. 'We'll have to stop it!'

'But how? How can people like us stop that sort of thing?'

'It's just a proposal, isn't it?' said Megan. 'The Council have to agree to let them do it.'

'Those bastards,' muttered Mr Fisher. 'They wouldn't stop a nuclear power plant if it brought them money.'

'If the Council lets them do it then we can appeal!' said Megan fiercely.

Luke stared at her. He'd never seen her like this, taking charge. It was almost as though she'd been half hidden behind a ... a tree or something, and he were really seeing her for the first time.

'Appeal to who?' asked Patrick.

'To the — what's it called? — the Land and Environment Court. We did it in Studies in Society last term.'

'Did we?' asked Patrick.

'Of course we did! Don't you ever listen?' Megan crossed to her mother and hugged her hard. 'We can win this, Mum! I know we can!'

The soup boiled over. Luke pulled the saucepan off the stove. Suddenly he felt like an intruder.

'I ... I'd better go,' he said awkwardly.

'What?' Mr Fisher looked as though he'd forgotten Luke was there. 'Thanks for your help this morning, son,' he said vaguely.

'No worries,' said Luke. 'I ... I hope it all works out.'

He had just grabbed his jacket from the old sofa on the verandah when he heard someone behind him.

'Luke!'

Luke turned. It was Megan. She brushed the hair out of her eyes awkwardly.

'What's wrong?'

Duh! Luke thought. How dumb can you get? Her family's farm is threatened and you ask what's wrong.

But Megan just bit her lip.

'They ... they wouldn't have a clue how to fight this thing,' she said bleakly. 'Mum and Dad don't think about things outside the farm. Pat either. They don't know how things work.'

But you do, thought Luke. Patrick was a born farmer, but Megan? Megan would soar above the world.

Where had that thought come from? He stared at her. How come he'd never noticed what she was really like before? Had she changed, or had he? The idea shocked him so much he hardly heard her next words. 'Sorry?'

'I said ... Luke, please could you help us? You're different. I mean, you like farming like Pat, but you think about things too. Hell, I'm saying this all wrong —'

'Of course I'll help,' Luke broke in. 'I don't know what I can do, though,' he added honestly.

Megan took a deep breath. 'Could you ask Sam?'

'Ask him what?'

'To do something about us on his show? Explain why the resort would be such a bad thing. Please? It'd really make the Council stop and think if there was something on TV. It's not just us,' she added hurriedly. 'I mean, it's happening in lots of other places too — resorts or golf courses or silly trivial things taking resources, using up water. Did you know that one hectare of a golf course uses ten times more herbicide and pesticide than our orchard?'

'No, I didn't know,' said Luke, impressed.

Megan looked embarrassed. 'Sorry. Of course you wouldn't. There was a documentary on TV. My brain just seems to remember stuff like that.'

'I like it,' said Luke, then felt even stupider than before.

'Luke, if Sam says the resort's a bad idea the Council will listen to him. You know they will.'

Luke nodded. 'I'll ask him. He'll be back today.'

'Thanks, Luke. You're a real friend.'

'I'll do anything I can to help,' said Luke. He was surprised how much he meant it, not just for the Fishers, but for Megan especially.

He watched her as she went back inside.

Chapter 7

Luke

In thunder, lightning, or in rain
(*Macbeth*, Act I, Scene 1, line 2)

The cows stared at Luke as he walked back down the hill, still hoping that he'd magically produce a bale of hay from his pockets, then bent down to the cold grass again. He hardly noticed them.

How could things change so fast? The Fishers' place was the one thing that never changed, no matter what else happened in his life. And now this ... But maybe Megan was right. If Sam just spoke up for them on the show, the Council would be forced to stop the resort ...

The four-wheel drive was parked in the courtyard when he reached home.

Mum's voice floated out of the kitchen window.

'*Mountains hiii ... iiighhhhh ...* Something something *coming home, Mountains hiii ... ighh ...*'

Luke grinned. Mum's singing sounded like one of the cows in trouble. But at least it was easy to know when she was happy.

The house smelled of roast beef. 'Our own meat,'

Sam boasted whenever they had anyone to dinner. 'You won't find better beef in the world.'

'Is that you, darling?' Mum came out of the kitchen, wiping her hands on her jeans. They'd been new the week before, but Luke noticed there were already stains at the knees.

'Yeah, it's me,' he replied. 'How was Sydney?'

'Okay,' said Mum vaguely, 'except I forgot to change my shoes when I got out of the car at the airport. So there I was with my gumboots under my dress at the TV station!' She eyed him more closely. 'Hell's bells, you look like you've been dragged through a hedge backwards.' She picked a twig out of his hair.

'I've been pruning. Over at the Fishers'.'

Mum'd had her hair done again in Sydney. The colour was different somehow. Luke squinted then worked it out: red streaks among the brown and blonde. But she'd managed to make a mess of it already.

He bent down and kissed her cheek while she hugged him. It felt strange to bend down to Mum, when only last year he'd still had to reach up.

'How are they? It's been donkey's years since I've been over there . . .'

'Mum, they're really upset. Someone's going to build a —'

'A resort? Yes, I know.' Mum ran her hands through her hair. They were interesting hands, scarred and marked from her work with the cows. Mum might have streaks in her hair these days, but her hands never changed.

'Someone down in Sydney was saying something about a new resort up here.'

'You *knew*! Why didn't you say anything?'

'There wasn't anything to say. Not really. Just rumours. You know how things get about.'

'But ... but aren't you worried? All those people ...'

Mum went back to the kitchen and started to stir something on the stove. 'It won't affect us much, not on this side of the mountain. We might even get a regular air service from it.'

'But what about the Fishers? Mr Fisher says it'll ruin them.'

'What? Don't be silly, darling. You're exaggerating. It won't be that bad.'

'But what about the water?'

'What water?'

Luke sighed. How could Mum be so dense? 'The water the resort will use! They're going to have a golf course and ... and everything. Their water will come from the Fishers' creek.'

Mum stopped stirring and stared at him. 'Hell's bells and buckets of blood! I didn't realise!'

'Of course it'll probably be okay,' said Luke hurriedly. The last thing he wanted to do was worry Mum. He suddenly remembered the day Anderson's in town had told her it'd take a thousand dollars to fix the car and she'd had to leave it there; he'd never forget that look on her face as they'd hitched back home together ...

They'd been through a lot together, he and Mum.

'Megan's got an idea,' he added. 'She thinks if Sam can put something on his show the Council won't approve the development.'

'Maybe.' Mum looked uncertain. 'But lobbying the Council is a good idea. I'll give the Fishers a ring after dinner. The more people who can start ringing up and writing letters the better. We can do a ring-around . . .'

'Mum, there's no need to get worked up about it. I'm sure it'll be fine. What's for dinner?' he asked, to change the subject. It was always a formal dinner in the dining room on Sam's first night home.

'Chocolate mouse,' said Mum. Mouse, mousse. It was a family joke.

'Good,' said Luke. 'Where's Sam?' he added. 'I'll ask him about the Fishers now.'

'On the verandah.' Mum glanced at her watch. 'I'm just going to check the calves. Sometimes I think they could turn into beetles and Mr T wouldn't notice. Like to run down with me?'

Luke shook his head. 'I'd better talk to Sam. Then you can tell the Fishers it's all fixed.'

'Yes.' Mum still had that strange look of uncertainty. But then she nodded. 'You talk to Sam!' The door shut behind her as she went out to check the cows.

Sam was sitting watching the rosellas clamber about the bird feeder that hung on the verandah post. A magazine sat on the table next to him, with half a cold cup of coffee, but Luke doubted that he'd been reading. Sam always spent the first few hours at home just sitting. 'Letting Sydney slide away,' he put it.

He glanced up at Luke and smiled. It was his 'being friendly to the public' smile, the one that looked so good on camera. Sometimes, thought Luke, it was as though it took a while for the real Sam to take over from the public one. 'Hi, mate. Take a seat.'

Luke sat down.

'Sam . . . can I ask you something?'

'Of course,' said Sam. He looked surprised at the seriousness in Luke's voice. But his forehead didn't wrinkle. Was that Botox? wondered Luke.

You read about TV stars having their lines Botoxed and collagen-injected these days. But it wasn't the sort of thing you could ask your stepfather about.

'I've been over at the Fishers'. This development company, they're going to —'

'Riverland Developments. I know all about it. Bloke I know told me down in Sydney,' said Sam easily. 'It'll change the town a bit. Pity. But these things happen.'

'Mr Fisher says it will ruin them! The resort will take all their water!'

'And they want me to put their case on TV,' Sam finished. 'Look, mate, do you know how many requests like that I get each day? I'd need to have a show four hours long to do even half of them.'

'But this is different!'

'Is it?' Sam took a gulp of cold coffee, pulled a face then put it down again.

'They're our neighbours! Our friends! If . . . if there was a fire or something they'd help us.'

'I'd help if there was a fire too.' (If you were here, thought Luke.) 'But this isn't the same thing.'

'Why not?' demanded Luke.

'It just isn't. Take my word for it, will you?'

'No! We've . . .' Luke struggled to find the words and discovered he was almost shouting. 'We've got to help the Fishers! I've known them all my life! They're good people, and they've done so much for Mum and me! This is our country! We can't let strangers take it just to play golf on.'

For a moment he thought Sam was going to yell back, or tell him why the resort would be a good thing. Sam shut his eyes for a moment instead. 'Luke, just shut up a moment, will you? I need to tell you something. Something about the real world.'

'What do you mean?'

'I can't help the Fishers. I'd like to. But I can't.'

'Yes, you can! You can —'

'Do you know who sponsors my show?'

'What do you mean?'

Sam sighed. 'Shows don't pay for themselves. Advertisers pay for them. Riverland Developments are owned by United Holdings. United Holdings own Fruit Bubbles cereal ...'

'And Fruit Bubbles advertises on your show,' Luke said slowly. 'But does that mean ... does it mean they won't let you say anything bad about their companies? But that's censorship!'

'It doesn't work like that, Luke. Of course they don't tell me what I can and can't say on air.'

'You just ... don't say things they won't like.'

'More or less,' said Sam matter-of-factly.

'But ... but that's lying.'

'Of course it isn't. I just stay away from certain topics. Sometimes you have to make compromises, mate. My show is good stuff. I'm telling people about things that matter. But if I want to get that stuff to air there are some things I can't talk about.'

'But stopping the developers is important!'

'Everyone's problems are important. But you can't help everyone.'

Luke felt the anger burn through him, then erupt. It was more than fury about the Fishers. It was everything that Sam had done — taking Dad's place, trying to make Luke into something he wasn't. And it was everything Sam hadn't done, the longing for the stepfather that might have been. The hero. The invincible . . .

'That's just a cop-out! Don't you even have the guts to —'

'I have as much guts as anyone in the industry! I'm just not going to risk everything I've achieved for —'

'You're a fraud!' yelled Luke. 'And I'm going to tell everybody! Wonderful Sam Mackenzie, who doesn't even have the guts to criticise the people who advertise on his show! I wonder what they'll think when —'

'Really? And what do you think people would say if they knew all about you? You're in no position to call *me* a fraud . . .'

Sam stopped suddenly. The silence seemed to echo across the verandah. The feeding rosellas chattered suddenly, as though to fill it up.

'What do you mean?' asked Luke carefully.

Sam shrugged. He lifted up his coffee again, then remembered it was cold and put it down. 'Nothing. I shouldn't have said anything.'

'But you did,' insisted Luke. He'd never known Sam to be as uncomfortable as this. As though he were ashamed. But all he'd said was —

'Do you mean I'm a fraud too?' asked Luke. It came out before he could stop himself.

Sam didn't respond.

'Answer me! I'm not a kid any more!' shouted Luke.

'Aren't you? Then act like it.' Sam stood up. 'I'm going for a walk before dinner.'

'The exam?' said Luke suddenly. 'That's what you mean, isn't it? St Ilf's?'

'Yes,' said Sam reluctantly. 'Look, mate,' he added hurriedly, 'it's not what you're thinking.'

'Did you pay someone?'

'Of course I didn't pay anyone. I just rang up one of the masters there, a bloke I was at school with. I mentioned you'd had a hard time, lost a lot of school when your dad was sick —'

'You leave my dad out of it!'

'I just said you might need some help and could they give you some idea of what you might need to study for the exam.'

'So they sent me the exam paper to get Sam Mackenzie's stepson into St Ilf's?'

Sam stared. 'You mean they sent you the whole exam paper? I just thought ... I meant just a question or two, to help you along ...'

'You made me a cheat,' said Luke hoarsely. 'Just like you.'

'Luke, I didn't mean ...' began Sam.

Did Luke believe him? Had Sam arranged for him to see the whole exam paper or just a few questions?

It didn't matter. Luke stumbled to his room.

Chapter 8

Luke

Son: What is a traitor?
Lady Macduff: Why, one that swears and lies.
(*Macbeth*, Act IV, Scene 2, lines 46–47)

Dinner was quiet. Luke avoided looking at Sam as he carved the roast beef, or even at Mum.

'How many potatoes?' asked Mum.

'Two,' said Luke. Did she know? Had Sam said to her, 'Hey, don't worry about dumb old Luke, I can get him into St Ilf's, no worries'?

No, he thought. Mum wouldn't have gone along with something like that. All her delight when he'd won that scholarship had been real. And if Luke told her now she'd be doubly hurt. She'd find out she had a cheat for a husband as well as for a son ...

'I was just explaining to Luke,' said Sam heavily, 'why I can't put the Fishers on the show.'

'Advertisers,' said Mum.

Luke looked at her, shocked. 'You knew? Why didn't you tell me?'

Mum looked startled at the anger in his voice. 'I thought Sam might still be able to do something.'

'Well, I can't,' said Sam shortly.

Mum glanced at him, then at Luke. 'Well, there are still lots of other things we can do,' she said a bit too brightly. 'Write to the paper . . . and the councillors. Maybe a letter to each one of them.'

Small stuff compared with what Sam could do, thought Luke. But there was no way he was going to attack Mum too.

How could she stand up for Sam like that?

'I'll get the chocolate mousse,' said Mum, looking from one to the other. She was beginning to sound worried.

Luke stood up. 'I'm not hungry. I've got homework to do.'

'One of the joys of being an adult,' said Mum, trying to stay cheerful, 'is never having to do homework again.'

Luke didn't reply.

The homework wasn't just an excuse. He *did* have homework: he still had to try and get through *Macbeth*. Maybe for once he wouldn't leave it all till Sunday night.

It was even sort of good to get away from real life into homework. To have something else to think about instead of Mum and Sam and St Ilf's . . .

How would Mum feel if she knew Sam had thought that Luke was such a loser he'd never get into St Ilf's by himself? If she knew Sam *and* Luke were cheats . . . because he *was* a cheat now, he realised. He'd been a cheat ever since he got the scholarship and said nothing about the exam.

Would Sam really tell people Luke had cheated if Luke spread it around that he was a fraud who wouldn't speak out about something his sponsors were doing? It would hurt Sam too, wouldn't it?

Or maybe he wouldn't have to tell them right out. Maybe he'd just hint. He'd say, 'Luke had a bit of help, you know', with a wink and a certain look on his face, and people would go, 'Oh yes, dumb old Luke. We always knew he couldn't have got a scholarship by himself.'

Luke shivered. He had to think about something else for a while. At least *Macbeth* was another world, four hundred years away from his problems of lies and cheats.

Luke picked up his copy of the play. It was getting easier to understand the language now. Maybe he was finally getting the hang of it. Some bits were almost pretty good. Like when Lady Macbeth was trying to get up enough courage to kill the King.

> *Come, you Spirits*
> *That tend on mortal thoughts, unsex me here,*
> *And fill me, from the crown to the toe, top-full*
> *Of direst cruelty! make thick my blood,*
> *Stop up th'access and passage to remorse ...*

Okay, people today didn't talk like that. Luke supposed they never *had* talked like that really. But it still sounded ... well, almost real, in spite of the weird way they spoke.

Maybe that's what makes it a great play, he thought suddenly. It feels like real life, even if it isn't.

He read for another fifteen minutes, slowly getting into the story. Macbeth, convinced by the witches that he will be king, will now do anything so he *is* king, even kill good King Duncan. But he's scared by the monstrous thing he's going to do. '*Is this a dagger, which I see before me ...?*' he cries. '*Come, let me clutch thee ...*' After he kills the King he's in shock, so Lady Macbeth has to grab the dagger and smear the blood over the drunk grooms who are sleeping in the King's room, so it will look like they're the guilty ones.

Luke sat back. So that was what Mrs Easson had meant when she gave him 'Macbeth's Progress into Villainy' as a topic for his talk. Macbeth was an okay guy to begin with. But he didn't have the guts to do what he thought was right. Every evil thing he did led to another one ...

He put the book down, changed into his pyjamas and put a DVD in the machine. It was a new one that Mum had brought back from Sydney. She always brought him something when she came back and left it on his bed — a new shirt, maybe (the last one was two sizes too small), or that goat's-wool beanie that stank of billy goat as soon as it got wet. It was like she was saying, 'See? I was thinking of you while I was away' without having to use the words.

He got into bed and switched the DVD on using the remote. But he couldn't concentrate. The DVD was ... empty somehow. Everything that had happened today overshadowed it. Even *Macbeth* was more vivid. And last night's dream ...

Luke turned off the TV and lay back in bed.

That dream world was the place to live. A place where things were clear. Where enemies wore helmets and carried swords instead of exam papers. Okay, people were hungry and life was hard in some ways. But things were simple too.

He wished there were some way he could dream it all again. You couldn't choose your dreams, could you? But that's what he needed to dream of. Courage, like that of the Mormaer. A stepfather you could trust. A simple world . . .

He shut his eyes.

Sleep . . .

Chapter 9

Lulach

What! can the Devil speak true?
(*Macbeth*, Act I, Scene 3, line 107)

And suddenly he dreamed.

It's too sudden, thought Luke vaguely. Dreams don't start like this. You drift into dreams.

This felt as if he'd been dropped into a bucket of water. The whole world changed, and so did he.

I'm Lulach again, thought Luke. Him . . . me . . . it's all mixed up. But what he sees, I see as well.

He was asleep in this dream too. But the bed was different — warmer, fluffier. It crackled as he rolled. Somehow he knew the mattress was filled with goose feathers. He could remember the old women plucking the dead birds out in the courtyard, his mother hanging the feathers in linen bags in the chimney so the smoke would kill any lice.

The sheets felt soft against his skin. They were linen sheets, from Ireland. The people of Alba had been colonists from Ireland hundreds of years ago, but the sheets weren't as old as that. They were his

73

grandmother's sheets, and had come with his mother when she married his father.

How can I possibly know all this? thought Luke vaguely. But he wasn't Luke. He was Lulach, asleep between sheets that had been washed on the rocks by the river, and left to dry and soften in the sun.

Lulach ... Lulach ...

'No, not Lulach!' The cry came from the room next door. It was his mother's voice.

'I have no choice. I have to take him.' The Mormaer spoke quietly, but the words came through the wooden walls nonetheless. 'Thorfinn demands to see him. If I don't bring him the meeting's off.'

Was Lulach dreaming or was he awake? Thorfinn, who'd killed his father ... For a moment the dream wavered into his old nightmare: his father's body, all black skin and grinning skull.

'Why does Thorfinn want to see him?'

There was no answer, or none that Lulach heard.

'Thorfinn wants to take him hostage! Please, for pity's sake! You can't take Lulach! I can't lose him too!'

'No one mentioned a hostage.'

'But if he asks — or demands — what will you do?'

'Trust me,' said the Mormaer gently.

Lulach woke up properly. The room was dark, the moon outside hidden by the clouds. The rath was silent; even the voices from next door were quiet now. There was just the noise of a rat in the roof, and an almost-cough from the next room, like the sound of someone crying.

But that's silly, thought Lulach, rolling over in bed. Mother sleeps next door. And mothers don't cry.

He slept again. Suddenly a hand shook him. 'Lulach! Lulach, wake up!'

'What is it?'

'Shh.' His mother held a candle. The dawn was a grey light through the window. There were grey smudges under her eyes too, as though she hadn't slept. 'You must get dressed. Quietly.'

She handed him his clothes. They were his best ones: the new léine Meröe's girls had woven for him, the deerhide cloak with the sheepskin collar.

Lulach began to struggle into his stockings. They were his best ones too, of red wool with yellow stripes. 'Why?'

'You have to go on a journey with the Mormaer.' Lulach noticed she didn't call him his stepfather. 'A secret journey. No, don't ask questions. Hurry.'

'Have the Norsemen landed again?' He tried to wake up properly. Someone had been talking about Thorfinn, hadn't they? Or had that been a dream? Maybe he and the Mormaer had to go and fight the Norsemen again, just like they had last month, he thought hopefully. The Mormaer would do another trick and they'd be heroes.

'No, nothing like that. Here, let me help you with your boots.'

'I can do them. Will you come too?' he added.

'No. I wish I could, but I need to stay here. Someone needs to take charge with the Mormaer and Kenneth gone.'

'Is Kenneth coming too?'

'Yes. Lulach . . .'

Lulach looked up from tugging on his boots. 'What?'

His mother hesitated, then bit her lip. 'Nothing. Just ... do what your stepfather tells you to. Understand? No matter what he tells you to do. You have to trust him.' She said the words almost like a prayer.

Lulach nodded. He wasn't sure what he was agreeing to. Trust his stepfather? He did already. The Mormaer was a hero. He'd taken Lulach hunting twice last month, high on his big horse, and let him hold his deer spears. Now the whole of Moray knew that Lulach would be his tanist, as soon as he was fourteen and a man.

The Hall was quiet as they crept down the stairs. The rath's unmarried men snored on their pallets by the fire; someone coughed from one of the bedrooms on either side. A dog got to its feet and looked hopeful, but sat again at the Lady Gruoch's silent signal.

It wasn't as dark outside. The sky was an arc of pewter-grey.

Three horses were stamping their feet outside the door, their breath white in the cold air. One was Lulach's pony, and the Mormaer and Kenneth were already on the other two. Lulach grinned. So he was to have his own horse today!

Lulach's mother tied the strings of his cloak more tightly, then pinned something at his collar. It was his father's gold brooch. It gleamed in the light of the candle. The Mormaer glanced down at it, but said nothing.

Lulach's mother hugged him hard and adjusted the collar of his cloak. 'God speed,' she said quietly.

Lulach waited for her to kiss his stepfather

goodbye too. But she didn't. She just said, 'Look after him.'

The Mormaer nodded. He spurred his horse. The others followed.

The sea and the fishermen's cottages were at their backs. They were heading inland. There was no track to follow here, just the river. Mist rose from it as the daylight grew, and a thin veil of white covered the hills as well. In a land with few roads, burns and rivers were the real highways. It felt grand to be riding his own horse with the two men, as though he were an adult too.

Where are we going? Lulach wondered. But if his mother wouldn't tell him, he guessed there was no point in asking the Mormaer either.

Gradually the sun rose: a thin slip of gold at first, then larger and larger, dragging the day's light with it. The hills turned green instead of grey, patched with bracken's gold and heather's purple. Bent trees shivered silver in the early sunlight, and ale-coloured streams crept between the hills.

At last they left the river and followed a smaller one, heading north. The air smelled of distant sleet.

'There's food in your saddle bag!' called the Mormaer. They'd been riding for hours now and Lulach realised he was starving. He reached down with one hand and fished inside the leather bag. There was a piece of oatcake, wrapped inside a scrap of linen, and a hunk of cheese leaking its grease into the cloth. He nibbled on the cheese as they rode, but left the oatcake. His mouth felt too dry to eat it. But he didn't like to suggest they stop for a drink.

The sun crept higher. Clouds gathered over the hills, then sped across the sky. It began to rain: sun showers that lasted for less time than you could sing a chorus, here then gone again.

Lulach pulled the hood of his deerhide cloak over his head.

The Mormaer glanced back at him. 'Not long now!'

The stream they'd been following was even smaller now. The Mormaer stopped at a burn that ran down from the hills, as though to check the way. Then he gestured to Kenneth. They headed off up the hill, leaving the river behind. Lulach spurred his pony to follow, weaving in and out of the heather. He hoped the pony wouldn't stumble on this rough ground. But they reached the top of the hill in safety.

A glen was spread out below them. Groves of trees grew in its shelter, a small loch edged with reeds and moss gleamed, shaggy cattle grazed on the hills. A field of barley glowed green behind a two-storey building, with a cattle byre behind.

It must be a guesthouse, Lulach realised. Every clan kept guesthouses throughout their territory, to give travellers free food and a bed for the night.

Lulach glanced up at the sky. The sun wasn't even at midday yet. Surely it was too early to stop for the night!

The three horses cantered down the slope. They stopped at the front door of the guesthouse and their riders dismounted. Lulach felt his knees tremble after so long in the saddle. His tummy growled too. It had been a long time since the piece of cheese.

The Mormaer smiled. 'Time to eat,' he said, ringing the guesthouse bell.

'Yes, yes, I'm coming!' An old woman shuffled out of the door then stared. She was Meröe's age, though there were more teeth in her wrinkled face. 'My Lord!' she gasped, as she recognised the Mormaer. 'Please . . . please enter. It's an honour . . . you'll want rooms, the bedding is all aired . . .'

'Just food, if you will.'

'Anything! My husband says I'm the best cook in the glen!' boasted the woman, standing back to let them pass.

Lulach glanced at the countryside around them. As far as he could see she was the *only* cook in the glen too.

The Mormaer bent his head under the lintel. Suddenly Lulach remembered his father telling him why doors were always low. 'That way you can chop off an enemy's head before he lifts it again,' his father had said. He'd laughed, but Lulach could tell that he was serious.

Why had he thought of his father now? Was it because he had heard the name Thorfinn last night?

Had he heard it? Or had it been a dream?

It was cool inside the guesthouse, despite the fire at the end of the long room. The Mormaer and Kenneth made their way towards it.

What were they all doing here? Lulach sat on the bench by the fire and watched Kenneth and his stepfather, trying to find a clue. The Mormaer was sitting on one of the benches too, looking as relaxed as if he were in his own Hall. But Kenneth was restless, pacing back and forth by the fire.

'You stay here with the boy,' said Kenneth abruptly. 'I'll scout around.'

'Thorfinn said midday,' said the Mormaer mildly. 'There'll be nothing to see yet.'

Thorfinn! Lulach started. So he hadn't been dreaming!

'If he keeps his word,' said Kenneth grimly.

'He will. He has as much to lose as we have.'

'Except the boy.'

Lulach started again. Did Kenneth mean him? What were they talking about?

The Mormaer shook his head. 'Lulach is no use to Thorfinn.'

'Then why does he demand to see him?'

'Who knows? But go if you like.'

Kenneth nodded. He strode out the door.

Lulach couldn't contain his curiosity any longer. 'My Lord . . . what's happening?'

'It's a meeting,' said the Mormaer. 'Thorfinn and —'

There were footsteps outside the door. Lulach glanced up. But it was just the hostel-keeper's wife hurrying in with more wood for the fire.

'There,' she panted, as the flames flared higher. 'Now, I'll just milk the cow. I've been leaving the calf to suck, but the cow's a grand milker. And there are chickens . . .'

Chickens were precious in these hungry times, but this was the Lord of Moray.

The Mormaer shook his head. 'A bannock and a bit of cheese will be plenty. Anything.'

'A bannock!' The woman looked disappointed that the Lord of Moray didn't want anything fancier than flat bread. 'I'll make them fresh! And cheese — green cheese or hard cheese?'

Green cheese was fresh cheese, soft and white. Hard cheese was kept to mature.

'Either,' said the Mormaer. 'Green cheese, if you like.' There was a hint of impatience in his voice — but only a hint, as though he guessed how few travellers the old woman had to talk to in these days of Duncan's wars.

'Green cheese then, my Lord,' prattled the woman nervously. 'And you'll have your bannocks quick as blinking.'

She bent down to feel the hearthstone, then looked relieved. 'The stone is hot already,' she chattered, as she scooped cold barley porridge out of the pot beside the fire, patted it flat then placed it on the stone to bake. 'It's a good thing I lit the fire this morning; with this warm weather we've only had it lit at night. It's almost like I knew you were coming!'

She hurried out again to get the cheese.

'If she knew we were coming,' the Mormaer said, half to himself, 'she'd probably have had half the neighbourhood here for a feast.'

'Sir?' said Lulach. 'You didn't answer my question.'

The Mormaer met his eyes. 'Thorfinn has asked for a meeting. A secret meeting, just himself and me, with one guard each.' He paused. 'And you.'

'Me too? Why?' He half hoped the Mormaer would say, 'Because you'll be my tanist. You're my appointed heir.'

But the Mormaer just shook his head. 'I don't know.'

Lulach was silent for a minute. Then he said, 'Sir? Will we kill him?'

The Mormaer smiled slightly. 'No.'

'But sir! He killed my father!'

'He's killed many men. But that was in war. War is different, Lulach. King Duncan started that war. It was Duncan who invaded Thorfinn's lands. Thorfinn was defending his country when he killed your father.'

'But . . . but my father was a hero!'

'Yes, your father was a hero. He fought for his king. But Thorfinn was defending his people. Some might say he was a hero too.'

'But they can't both be heroes!' protested Lulach.

The Mormaer smiled. 'Why not? Lulach, the land needs peace. We can't afford another starving winter. If I can reach agreement with Thorfinn there might be an end to all this insanity. If we can —'

The door opened again. Kenneth's bulk darkened the doorway. 'They're coming, my Lord,' he said quickly. 'One guard, as promised. No sign of any more.'

The Mormaer nodded. 'I thought so. Men call Thorfinn a murderer, but I have never heard that he broke his word.'

'Perhaps they didn't live to tell the tale,' said Kenneth. He looked at Lulach, watching eagerly by the fire. 'My Lord, leave the boy here, I beg of you. I'll stay with him, watch him. It will be too easy for them to snatch him, if things don't go well today.'

'The boy comes with me. He needs to know how things are done. And his presence will be a sign to Thorfinn that I trust him.'

Thorfinn, the Raven Feeder. The nickname ran through Lulach's mind. After Thorfinn's raids, the women said, the ravens grew so fat on the dead bodies that the land was black — burned featureless below, full of black birds above. Thorfinn the killer,

Thorfinn whose men tried to burn our lands, Thorfinn whom I vowed to murder one day . . .

But the Mormaer had said Thorfinn was a hero too.

Could there really be a world without war? Could the Mormaer really change things so that men like his father didn't have to die?

The Mormaer was watching him. 'Come on, lad.'

Lulach paused to pull up his stockings. He couldn't meet his father's murderer with wrinkled stockings. Then he followed the Mormaer, who was already striding out the door and calling to the hostel-keeper's wife that they would eat her fine food later.

The Mormaer walked across the green, cow-cropped grass, Lulach on one side, Kenneth on the other. Lulach felt for the dagger in his belt. It was a new one, a present from the Mormaer last Michaelmas. A dagger wouldn't be of much use against Thorfinn if he were armed, but it was a comfort all the same.

If they try to take me hostage I'll fight them, he promised himself. For a moment he imagined himself single-handedly keeping Thorfinn at bay, and all his men as well, while the Mormaer and Kenneth were already prisoners . . .

And then he saw them, far along the muddy road. A group much like theirs, with one man out front, his red hair bright as the flames in the hearth they had just left, like the Mormaer's, but bushier; he was broad as a bear and fat as a chicken after stuffing.

Thorfinn, thought Lulach. He looked too fat to be a hero. But he didn't look like a villain either.

The two groups drew closer together. Suddenly Thorfinn held up his hand. It too was fat. Rings sparkled on each finger.

At this signal his guard stood back. The big man walked on alone.

The Mormaer nodded to Kenneth. Now he and Lulach walked by themselves too.

The wind began to gust. It blew icy air onto their faces. The trees swayed like they were trying to swim into the wind. The sudden cold made Lulach's nose run. He wiped it on his cloak.

He and the Mormaer were only six lengths from Thorfinn now. He could see Thorfinn's stomach sway as he walked. Thorfinn's huge nose was crooked as a fish-hook.

The Norseman put one hand down to his scabbard and drew out his sword, while the other pulled a white-painted branch from his belt.

'Well!' he called. 'Which do you choose? The sword or the stick?'

The Mormaer smiled slightly. 'You called this meeting, Thorfinn. I choose the white stick of truce. What do you want to say so secretly?'

Thorfinn grinned. His teeth were long and very white. He slipped his sword into its scabbard again.

'I think you know. Your great King Duncan has started five wars in five years and lost them all.' Thorfinn's grin grew wider. 'Two of them were against me and my people. Now he's heading north to fight us again.'

Lulach's stepfather nodded. 'Well?' he asked.

'I've been told,' said Thorfinn slowly, 'that Alba's

chiefs asked Duncan to step down as high king. But he refused.'

'You're well informed.'

'If Duncan died in battle,' continued Thorfinn, 'you might be elected high king.'

'I might. Duncan's brother might too.'

'Face facts, man!' cried Thorfinn, rapidly losing patience. 'Duncan is *mad*! No one is going to vote for a madman, nor for his brother! The Moray Clan is as strong as Duncan's. The people will follow your lead!'

Lulach glanced up at the Mormaer. His face was expressionless, as though waiting for Thorfinn to say more.

Thorfinn flung the white branch down so hard that it broke. 'Admit it! Your people are starving! There are hardly enough men to bring your harvest in! Crops have been burned year after year!'

'And you've done much of the burning,' said the Mormaer grimly.

'Aye. War is war. But you and I could come to an agreement. Both of us against the King now. And afterwards, when you are king . . .'

'*If* I am king . . .'

'Neither to attack the other's lands. Moray and Orkney to come to each other's aid if one of us is invaded. I have trouble enough from Norway. The last thing I need is a land-crazed southern king snapping at my heels.'

'And that is all?'

'One more thing. When you are king . . .'

'*If* I am king . . .'

'When you are king, your son to marry my daughter. Well, what do you say?'

Son? thought Lulach stupidly. He means me! That's why he wanted to see me, to make sure I'm not lame, or a halfwit. He wants me to marry his fat, ugly daughter!

Lulach watched as his stepfather held out his hand.

It began to rain.

Chapter 10

Luke

By the pricking of my thumbs,
Something wicked this way comes.
(*Macbeth*, Act IV, Scene 1, lines 44–45)

The bus was late. Luke stamped his feet as he waited at the gate, trying to keep warm. The bus was always late. One day, Luke thought, it'll be on time and half the kids will miss it.

He couldn't get Saturday night's dream out of his mind. It had been even more vivid than the first time. But different too.

Things hadn't been as simple back in Lulach's time as he'd first thought. Someone like Thorfinn might start off as your enemy and then become your friend, or at least your ally. For some reason something Sam had said on Saturday night came into his head. 'Sometimes you have to make compromises, mate.'

Nah, thought Luke. That's different. The Mormaer was protecting his people. Sam just thought about his precious job.

What had happened next? Had the Mormaer become king? Had Thorfinn kept his word? he wondered.

Luke had hoped the dream would come again last night, but it hadn't.

It *was* just a dream, he reminded himself, as the bus rounded the corner and pulled up in front of him.

Mrs Reynolds was driving. She smiled at Luke, showing a few too-white false teeth next to her yellow real ones. 'Saw your stepdad on TV this morning. He really gave the Prime Minister what for. Politicians should tell us what they're really going to do when they're elected! Can't trust them as far as you can throw them, in my opinion. You tell Sam from me he's doing a great job.'

As if! thought Luke as he made his way down the bus. Old witch, old shark, old velociraptor. When Mum had been really broke, Mrs Reynolds hadn't even let her ride on the school bus so she could take that checkout job in town.

What was that bit in the play? *Double, double toil and trouble: Fire, burn; and, cauldron, bubble.* That was Mrs Reynolds, all right. She probably had a cauldron in her laundry and went out at midnight stealing stray dogs and hacking bits off black snakes ...

'Luke! Oy! Luke!'

Patrick was waving from the back of the bus. Megan was sitting beside him.

'What were you dreaming about?' demanded Patrick, as Luke sat down next to him.

'Oh, nothing,' he said.

'What did Sam say?' asked Megan eagerly. 'Will he put our case on TV?'

Luke hesitated. Why wouldn't the words come? He wanted to say, 'The bastard won't do it. He's scared of what the advertisers will say.' But what if Patrick told someone else? And they told a reporter and it got into the papers? Hurting Sam meant hurting Mum. And Sam could hurt him now too.

What would Pat and Meg think when they heard the truth? Maybe they would think he just hadn't tried hard enough to convince Sam to help them. But how could he argue with Sam while his own grubby secret was hanging over him?

Coward. And Patrick and Megan were still waiting.

'I ... I asked him. He said he'd see what he could do.' The words came out before he realised he was saying them.

More than a coward. Liar. Cheat.

Again.

Megan beamed. 'That's fantastic!'

'You're the best!' said Patrick.

'No, really.' Luke tried to backtrack. 'He may not be able to do anything! The producer has to agree. Maybe they just won't think it's interesting enough for the whole country.'

'They will,' said Megan confidently. 'There must be things like this happening all over the place, not just here. Big developments forcing people out, using all the resources ...'

'Yes, but ...'

The bus stopped again and more kids got on. 'Hey, Jingo!' called Patrick.

Jingo lumbered down the bus. 'Hiya!' he said, dumping his bag at Luke's feet. 'Heard your dad asking the Prime Minister about terrorists this morning.'

'Stepdad,' corrected Luke.

'Whatever.' Jingo glanced at Megan, then pretended he hadn't. But his voice grew louder as he deliberately didn't look her way.

Huh, thought Luke. Showing off.

'We should just nuke them, dude,' he announced. 'That'd show them!'

'Nuke who?' demanded Megan.

'Those Iraqis,' said Jingo. 'They're all terrorists, aren't they? Get rid of the lot of them.'

'Why? Aren't we supposed to be liberating them? How can you nuke someone and liberate them at the same time?'

Luke grinned. He knew Megan really meant it. She wasn't just showing off back at Jingo.

'It was all a lie, anyhow,' said Megan, shoving her hair out of her eyes. 'All that stuff about the weapons of mass destruction.'

Jingo shrugged. 'So? Saddam Hussein was a crook and we went in and got rid of him. What does it matter what it took to get us in there?'

'But it wasn't true!' objected Megan.

'Yeah, okay. But what if everything's better because he's gone?' argued Jingo. 'The Iraqis have elections and stuff now. What if everything works out for the best and they finally have peace after all these years? Isn't it worth a few lies?'

'Politicians say stuff that isn't true all the time,' Luke put in. 'Or they use spin doctors to try to make things sound better than they really are.'

'That doesn't make it right!' said Megan.

'Why not? I bet you say things that aren't true,' insisted Luke.

'I don't!'

'I bet you do! Like on Saturday, when you said you couldn't remember what "will" meant in Shakespeare's time. I bet you could.'

'What *does* it mean?' Jingo actually sounded interested, not like he was just showing off.

'Something rude,' said Luke. 'But Megan won't say.' He turned to Megan again. 'Look, I bet you'd tell Briony her haircut was cool even if she looked like a loser.'

'But that's different!' insisted Megan. 'That's ... that's just so I don't hurt her feelings!'

Suddenly it seemed desperately important to prove to her that some lies were okay. 'Yeah, well, I bet that's what politicians say. "It's just to make people feel better. It's just so we can get into power and get some good things done." That's how they win elections.'

Megan was silent for a moment. Luke was worried he'd offended her.

But then she said slowly, as though she'd really been thinking, 'Maybe you're right. It's not just black and white, is it? There are times when it's okay to tell a lie. But sometimes you *know* it's wrong, when truth really matters.'

'Maybe it's only okay to tell a lie when it doesn't hurt someone. If you think you're doing it for a good reason,' said Patrick suddenly.

Luke blinked at him. It wasn't like Patrick to think about things like that.

Patrick shrugged as everyone looked at him. 'It's just what Nanna used to say,' he said. '"It's only all right to lie when you don't hurt anyone." That was when I put a cow's tooth under my pillow for the tooth fairy ...'

The bus pulled up outside the school.

Chapter 11

Luke

Not in the legions
Of horrid Hell can come a devil more damn'd
In evils, to top Macbeth.

(*Macbeth*, Act IV, Scene 3, lines 55–57)

Luke stared out at the pigeons strutting around the garbage bin, then forced his attention back inside the classroom. He tried to concentrate as Mrs Easson read from *Macbeth*.

He didn't mind the play now — bits of it were good, he'd decided. But it was all so far away from what was really on his mind. This morning's conversation kept going round and round in his head.

Maybe lies *were* all right if they didn't hurt anybody. And no one was hurt by his winning the scholarship, were they? Except maybe the kid who *would* have won the scholarship. Luke thrust the thought away. Mum was happy, Sam was happy; the only person really hurt was him. He'd have to go to St Ilf's now.

Maybe if he really worked he wouldn't do too badly there. Maybe Mum was right and he wasn't dumb, he'd just lost so much school with Dad being sick.

Everyone lied sometimes, didn't they? So what did one more matter?

And what about the lies you didn't actually tell? Sam pretending that he made up everything he said on air but really only saying what someone else had written for him. Politicians not mentioning what they *really* planned to do after an election. Was there such a thing as a lie that wasn't there?

He'd never actually *lied* about the exam, had he? He just hadn't said, 'I had the answers all prepared.' None of it was his fault, he hadn't wanted it to happen. So maybe . . .

'*"Aroynt thee, witch!" the rump-fed ronyon cries,*' read Mrs Easson.

What's a 'ronyon'? wondered Luke.

Maybe Shakespeare wasn't as out of it as he'd thought. Shakespeare seemed pretty sure about lies, at any rate. Evil people like witches lied, Macbeth lied. Good guys like King Duncan told the truth. Hey, that was one of the names out of his dream, wasn't it? There'd been a King Duncan, just like there'd been witches (or old ladies with beards, anyway).

So what? That's what you did in dreams, he supposed. You mixed up real things with dumb things, like being able to fly.

He glanced over at Megan. Her eyes were on her book. But somehow she had lost some of her brightness since last week.

She's really worried about the development, he thought. And now I've lied about that too.

Lulach's stepfather would have raised an army to drive the developers out, or thought of some cool trick to get rid of them. But he was just dumb old Luke . . .

There had to be some other way he could help the Fishers!

Chapter 12

Lulach

Where are they? Gone? — Let this pernicious hour
Stand aye accursed in the calendar!
(Macbeth, Act IV, Scene 1, lines 133–134)

It was Tuesday night: two days of lying at school. No, not lying, Luke told himself as he lay in bed and watched the moonlight make shadows on the wall. Just not telling all the truth . . .

Funny, he'd always hated going to bed before. But now sleep was a refuge.

Well, not just sleep. The dream.

It was like having your own virtual-reality machine. Somehow he knew he would vanish back to that world tonight, even though the dream hadn't come for two nights now.

Lulach's world was turning out to be more complicated and interesting than he'd thought. If only he had a stepfather like the Mormaer, instead of Sam . . .

Luke shut his eyes. And waited.

The world changed. The sounds changed. The caw of the rooks in the roof of the Hall, the *snick snick snick* of sickles slicing through the ripe stalks of barley all around him.

Lulach stretched out his sickle and cut another armful of grain. Normally only women cut the barley. The men would tie it into sheaves and stack them to dry for threshing. The grain was kept for bread and stews, the bran to make sour fermented ale, and the straw for beds.

But once again there were no young men to tie the barley, or to cut the bracken to make beds for the cows in winter, so women had to do their jobs instead. It was only two months after the Mormaer's meeting with Thorfinn. But already the men had marched away to war again.

Men had marched away to war every summer of Lulach's life. But this time the men of Moray were fighting against King Duncan, not for him.

The clear sky stretched above him, with not even a bird to break the blue. Up on the hills above the fields the cows chomped and tore at the grass, lifted their tails and left their droppings, nudged their calves then ate some more. A cow's world never changes, thought Lulach. No matter what happens in the world of men, cows just keep munching grass.

Lulach's arms ached, and his back and knees as well. He was the youngest child working in the field today. Even Knut was gone now, to study at the monastery.

The women were silent as they swung their sickles. The older women spinning on the doorstep of the Hall had stopped their gossiping. It was as though war had sucked away their songs as well as all their men, and all the women could do was wait till the battle spat them back. *Will he return? And how? Blinded? Scarred? His arm hacked off by a broadsword blow?*

It would soon be the time of the feast when lots were drawn to see who would farm what bit of land over the next year, and which bits would be farmed communally to help the poor and sick. But no one had the heart for a feast now. What would they feast on, with the men away and no one to hunt or fish?

Something on the horizon caught Lulach's attention. He straightened and squinted into the distance. The speck on the road grew larger.

A runner, coming this way! In this world of mountains and few roads a man on foot could take a message as fast as one on a horse.

Lulach felt his heart leap like a salmon in the river.

The women had seen the runner too. One gave a cry, then clapped a hand to her mouth, as though the cry might bring bad luck.

A runner meant news. News of the war. News of their men.

Was the battle lost or won? How many would come home this time?

The runner was nearing the field now, his feet and legs bare beneath his smock, loping steadily along the muddy track. As he passed them Lulach thrust his sickle into a sheaf and ran after him.

The runner nodded to Lulach, but didn't stop. He looked flushed with tiredness, and dust mingled with his sweat. But it took all of Lulach's strength to keep up with him.

'What news?' he panted.

'My news is for the Lady Gruoch.' The runner's voice was almost too soft to hear. He had learned how to keep his breath for the run.

'I'm her son!'

'Then you'll hear the news soon enough — if you don't make me waste my breath by talking.'

'But ...' Lulach shut his mouth and tried to keep up as they ran through the courtyard and up to the Hall. But his brain was pounding even faster than his legs.

Was the battle over? Had they won or lost? Was his stepfather all right? Surely nothing could ever happen to a man as brave and strong as he was ...

A sudden vision of his father's blackened skull flashed before him. His father had been strong too ...

Women ran towards them from the fields, from the cow yards, the dairy. 'A runner! A runner's come!'

The Hall door was open, to let in light. Lulach followed the runner inside as his mother hurried from the storeroom. Her hands were clenched so hard the knuckles were as white as her apron.

'What news?'

The runner stood panting. 'Victory, my Lady.'

'Thank goodness. Oh, thank goodness.' The Lady Gruoch's face lost half its tension. 'And the Mormaer?'

'Unhurt, my Lady.'

'Ah.' It seemed to Lulach that his mother grew softer all at once, as though the strings that had held her taut were suddenly cut. She must really miss him, he realised suddenly. He had always thought that his mother had married again because it was her duty. But no one looking at her face could think that now.

'My Lady, there is more news. The King ... King Duncan is dead.'

Gruoch nodded, as though she had expected the news. 'How?'

'In battle, my Lady.'

'By whose hand?'

'Thorfinn, Earl of the Orkneys. Thorfinn challenged the King to combat. The King tried to flee, but Thorfinn slew him anyway. Once the King was dead the field was ours.'

'Duncan fought and fled too often. His men would have had little heart for battle,' his mother said, seemingly lost in thought. 'Well said and well run,' she told him at last. 'Meröe, get bread and mead for the runner, and whatever else he wants.' She hesitated, then pulled a bracelet from her wrist. It was twisted silver and had belonged to Lulach's grandmother. 'And this is yours, to thank you for the news.'

'My Lady.' The runner bowed his head, his hand clutching the bracelet.

Lulach looked around the Hall. Women had crowded all around to hear the news, so many they shut out the light from the door.

Why didn't they cheer? he wondered, watching their silent faces. Why didn't the women wave their scarves, as they had when the Mormaer tricked the Norsemen? They had won, hadn't they? The King was dead!

Now there would be no more wars! The Mormaer had vanquished war, just like he'd vanquished bad King Duncan!

Why were they so still?

He soon found out.

The men began to return three days later. When they left there had been great fanfare — but there were no songs now, no drums or pipers playing as they marched. These men limped, worn and starving. Armies lived off the land. But when they crossed the land too often, the land had no more to give.

Women ran to meet them with tears of joy. Children hid their faces in their mothers' skirts when their fathers no longer greeted them with laughter, but with blank expressions and hollow eyes.

Other women watched, searching the faces of the men for husbands, sons, brothers, friends. Sometimes they moved among the limping men, asking, 'Have you seen him?' 'Is he hurt — or did he fall?'

But mostly they just waited, wanting to keep their hope alive just a little longer.

Lulach kept his eyes on the road. But there was no sign of the Mormaer riding his horse high above the limping men.

The first to come home were tired, nothing more. They were the ones who could walk.

The next day brought the wounded: men who could still hobble, if their comrades helped them, with wounds that gaped and oozed despite being wrapped in bloody rags, or eyes gouged out by a sword. The women ran for fresh herbs and bandages.

And still the Mormaer didn't return.

The third day was the worst. Men on stretchers, carried by their friends. Bodies huddled together in an ox cart, still and bloody, with flies crawling on their wounds — so impossibly maimed it seemed that they were dead, till one man groaned and you knew that he, at least, still lived.

And then Lulach saw the Mormaer. He rode with his guard, high on their horses. Lulach stared at him. He was unhurt, just as the runner had said, though his face was thinner and there were shadows under his eyes. But there was something more.

The Mormaer led another horse, carrying the body of a man. Lulach stared. Was it a body? How could a corpse sit in the saddle, staring out with . . . with . . .

Lulach thought he would be sick. No, it wasn't a corpse. It was a man with half a face, one eye gone, the skin around it a burned red scar.

His stepfather reined in his horse, dismounted, then helped the wounded man down. The scarred man moved as he was guided, but nothing more.

A woman screamed in the doorway of the Hall. It was Meröe. Lulach had never thought that she could scream like that. Suddenly he realised why. The man was her son.

Kenneth.

How could any man look like that and live? What had Kenneth lived through, that would turn him into that?

Another woman ran from the cheese room, her hand pressed into her mouth to stop her sobs. Kenneth's wife. She and Meröe took Kenneth's arms. He stumbled between them to the Hall.

Lulach was dimly aware of his mother greeting her husband, of his stepfather saying something, anything . . .

And then he ran.

Ran to the hill, to the chomping, normal cows, and lay among the heather and the cattle droppings, surrounded by the familiar smells of dirt and cow. Anything to get away, to wipe out the stench of blood and death.

He lay face down, sobbing, till he heard a sound above him.

He looked up. It was a curlew, high in the sky. How many times had he called to a bird with Kenneth's pipes?

He sat up and pulled the pipes from his pocket. The bone was shiny now, from years of rubbing by his fingers. He put it to his lips and blew.

High above him the curlew called back, rising higher and higher in the sky.

At last Lulach put the pipes down. Tears still rolled down his cheeks. But they were easier now.

'Lulach.'

It was his mother. She must have come up the hill behind him.

'Go away!'

'Lulach, come back. It's your duty.'

Lulach shook his head. 'I don't care. Kenneth did his duty and look what happened!' The sobs were shaking him again.

His mother hesitated, then sat on the cow-cropped grass beside him. 'Your father said it was a sword thrust. It went right though Kenneth's helmet into his head.'

'But a sword cut doesn't look like that.'

'No. But he was dying. They had to burn the cut with a red-hot iron to stop the bleeding.'

'And now he has no face!'

'But he has his life,' his mother said softly. 'Your father said Kenneth struggled when they tried to lie him on the cart. He insisted on riding. One day, perhaps, he'll understand the world again. And Meröe will have her son and his wife her husband.'

Lulach shook his head. 'It's the Mormaer's fault,' he said hoarsely. 'He agreed to fight with Thorfinn. He said there'd be no more war! But this war was worse than any of the others!'

'Was it?' asked his mother quietly. 'You've seen men come back from war before. Maybe this one seems worse because you're growing up.'

'But ... but the Mormaer started this war! Duncan started the others, but this one was the Mormaer's fault!'

'If your father hadn't taken our men to war this time, Moray would have had to fight again anyway, with Duncan, against Thorfinn. We'd probably have lost again. Even more men would have died.'

Lulach didn't reply.

His mother hugged her knees, staring down at the Hall. Lulach suddenly wondered if she had ever sat on a hill like this as a girl, watching the cows, waiting for the news of war. Then, as though she read his mind, his mother said, 'I was your age when my father died, fighting King Malcolm's wars. I saw my brothers, then your father, die fighting for King Duncan. Lulach, I could have been mormaer here when your father died. I could even have stood against Duncan when they elected him king. But I knew that I could never send men to war.'

'Then you *should* have been mormaer!' said Lulach fiercely. 'That way Kenneth would have been safe!'

His mother sighed. 'No, Lulach. Most times war comes to you. There's no escape. Sometimes you have to fight. Your stepfather has protected Moray better than anyone else could have. I knew that when I married him.' She touched his hair lightly. 'And now perhaps there'll be no more war for any of us.'

Lulach shrugged. The future was far away. But the man with half a face was here and now.

His mother continued. 'Do you know who the true heroes are?' she asked him softly.

Lulach refused to answer.

'The ones who hate what they have to do, but do it anyway. It's called duty, Lulach. Duty is watching your husband ride away and wanting to scream at him, "Don't go!" But you don't scream at him. You hold the words back. Duty is waiting, smiling so no one sees your terror, making sure the cows are milked, the sheep are shorn, the fish are dried, so that there is something for the men to come back to. And when they do come back ...' She bit her lip. 'Lulach, do you love Kenneth?'

Lulach look up, surprised. 'Of course!'

'If you were Kenneth, what would comfort you the most? A boy who ran away from you? Or one who schooled his face and helped him? That's duty, Lulach. Doing what you have to do, no matter how hard it is.'

There was silence on the hill for a while. A hare peeped out from a clump of heather, its ears twitching.

'Did I hurt Kenneth, running away?' asked Lulach at last.

'He didn't notice,' said his mother gently. 'Not this time.'

She stood up and held out her hand to him. 'Come on, Lulach. You're going to be the Tanist of Moray. The people need to see that you care about them.'

Lulach looked up at her. 'I don't want to be tanist. I ... I want to study, like Knut. I want to go to the monastery too.' The idea had just come to him. But it seemed so good suddenly, to live among books, away from all the decisions of the world ...

'No,' said his mother shortly.

'Why not?'

'Oh, Lulach, how can I make you understand? You have no brothers, no cousins or uncles. Anyone else who could stand for election as mormaer is dead. There's only you. The clan must have a leader. The land must have a chief to tend and guard it.'

'And there's only me?' said Lulach slowly.

'There's only you.'

'Duty,' said Lulach. It seemed the heaviest word in all the world. 'If ... if you have another son, can I be a monk then?'

'Perhaps,' said his mother softly, smiling slightly. 'If I do.'

Lulach stood up, and followed her down the hill.

Duty, thought Luke, only half awake, a world and an age away from the small boy on the hill. How lucky to have someone to tell you clearly what your duty was.

And now the Mormaer would be king.

Or would he?

Luke rolled over and let the dream claim him again.

Chapter 13

Lulach

All hail, Macbeth!

(*Macbeth*, Act I, Scene 3, line 48)

The King was dead. It was time to elect another.

Down in England the king's son became king when his father died, even if he was evil or a fool. But here in Alba the mormaers and the bishops met at Scone to elect one of their number as high king.

The three of them rode along the muddy road into Scone — Lulach, his mother and his stepfather. The men of Moray marched behind them.

Flakes of snow drifted from the low grey clouds and melted on their faces, and the horses' hot breath turned the cold air into mist.

Lulach stared. He had never dreamed that any town could be so much bigger than the rath at home. There were more houses than you could count! Whole streets of tanners, potters, coopers, cobblers, shield makers ...

Out from the houses, down from the hills, people ran towards them — men in ragged leggings, women with tattered skirts, hungry children with fingers blue from the cold and feet bound up in rags, cheering, cheering, cheering . . .

'Moray!' they yelled. 'Moray! Moray!'

A woman ran up to them, a cloth-wrapped bundle in her hands. It steamed in the frosty air. She thrust it at the Mormaer.

'For you, my Lord!' she yelled. 'Fresh baked!'

It was an oaten bannock, hot from the firestone. The Mormaer broke off a piece and ate it, smiling down his thanks, then passed the rest to Lulach and his wife.

Lulach tasted it. It was gritty and sour. The oat flour must have been old and full of weevils. But it was the best the woman had to give.

Lulach had wondered if King Duncan's subjects would hiss at them, or hurl the contents of their chamber pots at the man who had killed their king. But these people didn't mourn for Duncan. Instead they cheered the man they hoped would be their next ruler.

That morning, at the guesthouse where they'd stopped for the night, Lulach had heard his stepfather practising what he'd say to the assembled chiefs.

'Duncan gave you war and hunger,' the Mormaer had recited. 'Black fields, with nothing to harvest but ruined hopes. I will give you peace.'

And he would, thought Lulach, as they rode between the cheering crowds. The Mormaer always kept his word. Surely the Council of Chiefs would see that too?

The chieftains and church leaders argued for three days, while the candidates waited in the monastery guesthouse, carefully polite to each other.

There were many candidates, but only two who really had a chance of being elected: the leaders of the two most powerful clans in Alba. The Mormaer of Moray and the new Mormaer of Atholl, King Duncan's brother. Thorfinn had been right.

King Duncan's father, the Abbot of Dunkfield and the former Mormaer of Atholl, had been lobbying the Council to vote for Duncan's brother. Duncan's son was too young to stand for election.

But Alba had had enough of Duncan's clan and their wars. On the third day the herald called out the name of the Mormaer of Moray.

Lulach stood at the front of the crowd on Boot Hill with his mother. She wore her best yellow gown today, with a red cloak and scarf. There were tears in her eyes; the tears she hadn't let herself shed in the years of terror and sorrow fell now, from happiness, as they watched the Mormaer stride up to the ancient Stone of Destiny, Lia Fáil, his head bright in the sunlight, his face intent and sure.

The new king put his hands upon the golden sandstone rock. His voice was strong and clear. 'I swear by my honour and by Almighty God to defend the Commonweal of Alba. I swear to defend the happiness of her people.'

One by one the clan chieftains stepped forward and pledged allegiance to the new high king. Each carried a little soil from their homeland in the bindings of their boots. They emptied it into a small mound, then yelled the new king's name so loudly the ravens rose in a thick cloud from the battlements and squawked in protest at the noise.

'King Macbeth!'

'Macbeth MacFindleach! All hail!'

'Macbeth! All hail our King Macbeth!'

'All hail, Father!' cried Lulach, and heard his mother laugh beside him. It seemed right to call him 'Father' now.

The new king grinned. He swung Lulach up onto his shoulders so that all the crowd could see him.

'Wave, my son!' he urged him.

Lulach waved. The crowd roared their approval. 'Moray! Moray! Macbeth! Macbeth!'

This is how it should be, thought Lulach. This is right.

No!

The dream shimmered as Luke struggled to wake up. This *wasn't* right! It *couldn't* be!

Suddenly the dream released him. Luke sat up panting, as though he had been running, not lying there asleep.

Not Macbeth!

That couldn't be the Mormaer's name! Macbeth was a murderer! How could he use Macbeth's name in his dream? Duncan, yes, even the three witches . . . but not Macbeth!

Luke lay back down. He had to think of another name for the new king. Arthur, maybe, or Jason. Did they have Jasons way back then?

He had to go back to sleep, he had to dream it right!

The King's name was . . . Samuel, that was a good name for a king. And all the people would cheer him and there'd be a feast ... and then he'd do something heroic again too ...

Luke shut his eyes and tried to see the dream again. But it was like playing with his action figures when he was small. You could move them all about but it wasn't *real*, not like the dream.

Real. The dream was *real*.

Suddenly certainty washed through him and his skin prickled. Whatever this dream was, it didn't come from him.

No dream he'd ever had before had been as clear as this.

How did he know what snow felt like? He'd seen snow on TV, but never felt it on his skin — so cold it hurt, then left you numb. How did he know what kale tasted like, boiled with seaweed in a pot? Or what a tanist was?

Where did the dream come from, then? Had he read a story like it, long ago, and then forgotten? But why would he want to read stuff like that? He wasn't even into history. And surely if he'd read all that he would remember!

It really happened, thought Luke dully. And I'm seeing it happen all over again!

But how? Why?

Maybe when things happened they left an echo. Like a yell travelling over a vast distance, until it was too faint to hear. Maybe, somehow, a distant ear could pick it up.

Maybe history never really dies, thought Luke, lying in the darkness and staring at the dim ceiling overhead. Maybe everything that's happened just waits for someone to listen to it again.

Somehow the darkness made it easier to think. Okay, suppose the dream *were* true . . .

But it *couldn't* be true, because the Macbeth he'd dreamed about was a hero. The real Macbeth was a coward and a murderer.

Except of course Shakespeare's Macbeth wasn't real either. Shakespeare's Macbeth was just a guy in a play.

Luke sat up again. *Had* it all happened? Then there'd be records. But how could he find out?

Now he was awake he was starting to think clearly. The same way he found out stuff for an assignment, he decided.

Google it.

Luke slipped out of bed. The computer sat dark and silent on his desk.

He pressed the power switch. The computer chimed as it booted up, so loudly Luke was sure that everyone in the house would hear.

What words should he key in? And then they came to him.

'Alba'. 'Tanist'. 'Duncan'. 'Moray'. 'Mormaer'.

Then, finally, 'Macbeth'.

Chapter 14

Luke

Show his eyes, and grieve his heart;
Come like shadows, so depart.
(*Macbeth*, Act IV, Scene 1, lines 110–111)

Dawn was a pale smudge between the curtains when he finally looked up from the screen. A cuckoo sang out in the loquat tree. Dad had told him years ago about the cuckoo, how it sang just before dawn, or even by moonlight sometimes. The kookaburra called next, then the rooster and all the other birds.

Luke turned off the computer. His body felt almost too heavy to move. He would be able to sleep now, he knew.

There were lots of sites that talked about Macbeth — too many for him to read them all. But he'd read enough to know the Macbeth he'd imagined was real.

The dream was true.

The real Macbeth had been a hero, just like in his dream. Then Shakespeare had written a play, making him a villain.

Shakespeare had called liars evil in his play. But it looked like Shakespeare had lied too.

And Lulach? Did he exist as well? Luke had typed in 'Lulach'. Most of the Macbeth sites didn't even mention him. But a couple of them said that Macbeth had married Gruoch, whose son became Macbeth's stepson . . .

Lulach. The boy he'd been.

Luke rubbed his eyes. Sleep. He had to sleep. Proper sleep, without the dream this time. There was no way he could read more now.

He knew enough already. Knew what was true and what was a lie.

Did it matter, any of it? And if it did, what should he do now?

Chapter 15

Luke

this dead butcher, and his fiend-like Queen . . .
(*Macbeth*, Act V, Scene 9, line 35)

It was a relief to meet Patrick and Megan later that morning, school bag on his back, Mrs T's banana and cheese surprise muffins heavy in his stomach. Even Mrs Reynolds's false teeth looked good, because they were familiar.

Normal, thought Luke. Part of him still felt trapped back in the dream. Green hills and purple heather, the yells of the crowd, the smells of chamber pots, the taste of ox roasted on a spit at the coronation feast . . .

'Hi,' he called, as he staggered down the bus, bracing himself as it bounced over potholes.

'Hi, yourself,' said Patrick gloomily. 'I have to go to the dentist this afternoon,' he added. 'I got a toothache last night. Mum rang for an appointment.'

'What time?' Luke sat down between the two of them.

'Two. At least I get the afternoon off school.'

'You'll miss English,' Megan observed.

'Yeah. I'm crying already,' said Patrick.

'No, I mean Mrs Easson asked you to read the part of Macbeth today, remember?'

Patrick shrugged.

'She should ask Jingo,' said Luke. 'He thinks he's king of the school.' He spoke without thinking. Dumb, he told himself. It sounded like he was jealous of Jingo. And he wasn't. Jingo was like a shiny bubble. One gust of wind and he'd evaporate.

Was Megan interested in Jingo? It was hard to tell what chicks felt. They'd been arguing yesterday. But sometimes girls pretended to be really down on a guy just because they liked him.

Megan didn't answer. Maybe she wasn't interested in Jingo, Luke thought hopefully.

Then she said, 'Luke? Has Sam said anything more about the TV show?'

Luke shook his head. 'I haven't spoken to him since he left for Sydney on Sunday,' he said honestly.

'Could you ring him tonight? Please? It's just that the Council is meeting next week . . . There isn't much time.'

Luke hesitated. Yes, he would call Sam, he decided. So what if Sam just said no again? At least he'd have tried. 'Okay,' he said.

Megan beamed at him. 'Thanks,' she said.

The school staff room was between the library and the Principal's office, part of the original school from more than a hundred years before. It was cold even on the hottest day, and dark unless the lights were on, the windows small and square in case those long-ago teachers needed to barricade out rebel convicts or settlers' kids who didn't like the idea of homework.

The staff room was full this early in the morning. As he knocked on the open door, Luke could see teachers gulping down final cups of coffee or photocopying notes on the machine in the corner.

'Mrs Easson, please,' he said, as the sports master looked at him inquiringly.

'What is it, Luke?' Mrs Easson came out into the corridor.

Suddenly he wondered how to start. He couldn't just say, 'I had this weird dream and wonder if it's real.'

'It's about Macbeth,' he said instead. 'I didn't want to bring it up in class because it's a bit embarrassing ...'

'Macbeth? Embarrassing?' Mrs Easson looked taken aback. 'What do you mean?'

'I ... I just had an idea last night. I looked up Macbeth and Scottish history and, well ... I found out something.'

'Yes?' asked Mrs Easson encouragingly.

'I ... I looked up the play last night, and it's all real!' He knew it wasn't coming out right, but he really needed to tell her what he'd discovered.

Mrs Easson looked puzzled. 'Yes, it's one of Shakespeare's history plays. Like *Julius Caesar* or *King Henry V*. We talked about that in class.'

'No, I don't mean that ...' Megan would know how to put it, Luke thought desperately. 'I mean, it's all a lie! Macbeth was real — Shakespeare didn't make him up. But he wasn't like that at all. Shakespeare lied about him. Macbeth wasn't evil, he probably didn't even kill King Duncan. And he didn't seize the throne, because Scottish kings were elected in those days, and people must have thought he was okay or they wouldn't have elected him. And Lady Macbeth didn't go mad, and —'

'Luke, hold it. It's just a play! It's not supposed to be true in all its details!' said Mrs Easson.

'But you just said it's a history play!'

'Yes, it's based on history and has historical figures in it. But it's still fiction.'

'But that's just it — it isn't! Shakespeare pretended he was writing about real people! But it was all a lie!'

'Luke, you keep using the word "lie". Fiction isn't a lie. A lie is when you deliberately change things.'

'Well, he did!' said Luke stubbornly. 'Shakespeare knew he was changing what really happened. So he lied.'

'All right, maybe he lied. But it doesn't matter! What's more important? A bit of forgotten Scottish history or one of the greatest plays the world has ever seen?'

'I don't know,' said Luke, confused now. 'The ... the play, I suppose.'

'Well, then,' said Mrs Easson, relieved. 'Of course, the history is very interesting,' she added kindly. 'I'm really impressed at all the trouble you're going to, Luke.'

'Thanks,' said Luke vaguely, his brain still far away. It wasn't enough that the play was brilliant, he thought. Surely it could have been brilliant *and* true. But he couldn't think how to explain that to Mrs Easson. Maybe if he were smart like Megan ...

But it was too late, anyway. 'There's the bell,' said Mrs Easson. 'See you in class this afternoon. Luke ... there's nothing else wrong, is there? Nothing at home?'

'What? No, why?'

'You've just been looking a bit worried lately. You must be excited after winning that scholarship, though.'

'Er, yes — everything's fine,' said Luke.

'Good.' Mrs Easson didn't look quite convinced. But she smiled at him, then went back into the staff room.

Chapter 16

Luke

Thou lily-livered boy.

(*Macbeth*, Act V, Scene 3, line 15)

School dragged all day.

Part of it was because Luke was tired from all that time on the Internet. But mostly it was because he was trying to think his own thoughts.

School wasn't a good place to think, Luke decided. The teachers kept getting in the way.

Was Mrs Easson right? Did the truth about Macbeth matter?

Maybe what she was saying was that lies didn't matter if good came out of them.

Shakespeare lied about Macbeth, but wrote a brilliant play. So that made it okay.

So what if he didn't tell anyone about the exam? He'd made Mum happy. Sam could boast about his stepson and Megan would think he wasn't the dumb kid next door after all.

He should just leave things as they were ... just enjoy people thinking he was great because he'd got a scholarship, enjoy the dream if it came back tonight ...

Things had turned out pretty well for Lulach, hadn't they? A stepfather he was proud of — and who was proud of him too.

What would happen next? he wondered.

No — what *had* happened next? All of it had already happened a thousand years ago.

Was there another war? What was Thorfinn's daughter like? Fat like him? Or maybe she was really hot. Perhaps she looked a bit like Megan, but with blonde plaits . . .

'Luke! Luke Beaton!'

'Wha — yes?' said Luke.

'We were talking,' said Mr Macintosh, 'about the square of the hypotenuse. Now, if Mr Beaton could just give us his valuable attention for a minute, we could all see that . . .'

I'll go back on the computer as soon as I get home, thought Luke. See if I can find out who he married.

He might even dream it tonight too — some of it, at least. But he wanted to know *now* . . .

'Luke!' said Mr Macintosh, exasperated.

It was funny listening to the play being read out that afternoon in Mrs Easson's class after he'd been living the whole thing. Especially with Jingo — Jingo! — reading the Macbeth part. There was no way Jingo could ever be a hero like the Mormaer, he thought. Except that in the play Macbeth was a villain.

'*Pr'ythee, peace*,' Jingo pleaded in his role as Macbeth, fed up with having his wife nag him to kill Duncan. '*I dare do all that may become a man; Who dares do more, is none.*'

Luke grinned for the first time that day. Maybe Mrs Easson had got it right. Maybe Jingo *was* like Shakespeare's Macbeth — a big man when his mates were around him. But Luke bet that Jingo wouldn't have the guts to do anything by himself.

'*What beast was't then, That made you break this enterprise to me?*' recited Megan. '*When you durst do it, then you were a man —*'

Mrs Easson held up her hand. 'Megan, Lady Macbeth is angry, she's trying to shame her husband into acting. She's even more evil than he is. Try to put more passion into it.'

Megan raised her chin. 'I don't think she's evil. She's just stuck with him and trying to make the best of it.'

'Interesting. All right then, that's your assignment for Friday. You can explain to us why you think Lady Macbeth isn't evil.'

Megan blinked. 'But I was supposed to talk about the poetic language!'

'I'm sure you can work out a new ten-minute talk,' said Mrs Easson easily.

Luke wondered if she was getting back at Megan for not agreeing with her. It was hard to tell with teachers. Sometimes they seemed to get off on your arguing, other times it just set them off.

He glanced at Megan. She didn't seem upset by the new assignment. Just thoughtful, as though she might actually *want* to do the extra work.

Mrs Easson looked at her watch, which got half the class checking theirs as well. Then the bell went.

Chapter 17

Luke

When shall we three meet again?
(*Macbeth*, Act I, Scene 1, line 1)

Luke lay in bed waiting for sleep, the smell of not-quite-roses all around him. Mrs T had sprayed his room again.

He'd been all ready to go back to the computer, to read more about what really happened to Macbeth and Lulach. But somehow he couldn't. He wanted to *live* it, not read about it.

Last night he had read about Macbeth's life. But his death would be there as well. Lulach's too.

Duh! Of course they're dead, dimwit, he told himself. It was a thousand years ago. You saw the dates last night. When Lulach was born, when he died.

But ... but he couldn't just *read* the rest of the story. It'd be like reading what his own life would be like: who he'd marry ...

... how he'd die.

No, he couldn't do it.

If the dream didn't come tonight, maybe ... maybe ... he'd look up more of the story then.

It was hard to get to sleep when you were waiting for it to come. Luke rolled over onto his stomach.

'Sleep ... sleep ... *Macbeth does murther Sleep* ...' The play's words kept sticking in his mind.

Maybe if he counted sheep. No, something Scottish. He tried to think. Haggises? No, they weren't animals, and anyway, he didn't know what they looked like. Bagpipes, perhaps ... or deer ...

There had been a deer in that first dream ...

Deer upon the hillside, a cluster of birch trees in a hollow, a brown stream running shallow through the grass, rocks weathered to strange shapes, their shadows waiting to pounce upon the white mist flooding up the gullies.

White mist ... no, thought Luke drowsily, not mist at all. The whiteness was sheep ... but close up they were more brown than white. He hadn't meant to think of sheep, but here they were ...

Chapter 18

Lulach

This castle hath a pleasant seat ...
(*Macbeth*, Act I, Scene 6, line 1)

The sheep ran down the track towards the stream.

'*Baa!*' they cried indignantly. '*Baaa!*'

They were small, with big horns and black faces and straggly wool.

'Head them back to the pool!' yelled one of the shepherds.

Finally the sheep were pushed into the water. They struggled across the pool and up the bank on the far side.

Kenneth laughed. 'There's nothing soggier than a wet sheep,' he said. Half his face was brown, the other puckered red. Kenneth must have recovered, just like Lulach's mother had said.

Lulach grinned. 'I imagine one of them will be our dinner at the abbey tonight.'

Lulach was much older — a few years older than Luke perhaps. Ten years or so must have passed, Luke realised. Other things had changed as well. These days Lulach wore fine woollen cloth, striped red and blue and yellow. His cloak was held with a silver brooch, and there were rings on his fingers. Even Kenneth wore gold rings now.

Their retinue rode behind them — guards, equerries (in charge of the horses), cup bearers, singers, pipers, even a troupe of jugglers in case the King got bored. Lulach had his own guard now too, and his own equerry — his old foster brother Knut, who had left the monastery the year before to join him.

It was a different land now too. The green hills were the same, and so was the soft dim sky. But the men who chased the sheep were young and well fed. They'd grown up in peace, not been starved in times of war.

Lulach and his men cantered on, leaving the shepherds and their flock behind but keeping close to the stream.

Long-haired black cattle grazed on the hills above them, like moving black boulders, and cloud shadows raced across the grass.

The stream grew broader and deeper. Fields stretched out on either side: barley, wheat and oats on the high lands, with kale, onions and leeks lower down. When the grain was harvested in a few months' time the cattle would be put to graze on the stubble.

The fields all belonged to the abbey — a gift from the King to enable the monks to feed the poor. No one starved during winter these days. Not under the rule of King Macbeth.

Lulach could see the abbey now: the big wooden main hall, the farm buildings, the church, the hospital with its separate building for the lepers, the high stone walls that would protect the herb beds, vegetable gardens and orchards from the harshest of the cold winds and, nearest of all, the lower stone walls of the community's guesthouse.

Tomorrow he'd be next to the King while he sat in judgment. Lulach looked forward to days like this. The King relied on the laws, of course, when he settled people's quarrels about inheritance or cattle theft. But he used his wisdom as well. Lulach thought he learned as much about his stepfather on such days as he did about the laws of Alba. And these days, he thought with pride, the King sometimes listened to Lulach's advice too.

Lulach had learned to read fluently these past few years. The laws that the people of Alba had brought over from Ireland were fascinating. Law was what protected the powerless, and made sure each person had equal access to land and care when they were sick. The law laid down how criminals should be punished. What other nations, Lulach sometimes thought with pride, had laws like these?

A gong sounded deep inside the abbey, a single stroke to mark the quarter hour, so that the neighbourhood would know what time it was.

Children ran to meet the royal party as they entered the abbey gate, laughing with excitement at the newcomers. One of the royal jugglers pulled a handful of knucklebones from his saddle bag. He tossed them in the air and caught them in a cascade while the children squealed with delight.

Out in the fields, their parents, the tenants of the abbey lands, stopped and waved or cheered.

'God bless our king! God bless our King Macbeth!'

It's a land of law and children now, thought Lulach, as they rode up to the abbey gate. If there was smoke on the wind these days it was from hearth cakes cooking or baking fish, not burning crops.

Even the seasons had been kind, men said, in these golden years of King Macbeth.

Lulach had been right. The guesthouse dinner was a grand one. Roast mutton as predicted, roast beef, roast swan, a giant salmon baked in a wicker basket over the fire, stuffed herrings, stewed eels from the abbey ponds, fresh heather ale, puddings of leeks and almonds or mushrooms with green cheese, oatcakes and fresh wheat bread.

The Abbot himself was fasting and didn't join them at the feast. Lulach sat at the High Table next to the King. No one approached the High Table unless the King beckoned. That small distance was the only privacy the King had these days.

The pipers finished their tune and began another, while a team of jugglers ran in, tossing their batons to each other. Lulach reached for a hunk of salmon. The juice dripped onto his trencher and he licked his fingers. He offered some to the King.

Macbeth took the fish absently. He had spoken little all through the meal. Suddenly he said, 'I got a letter last se'enight.'

'Sire?' The King received many letters, ten or more in a month, from lords or envoys abroad — even from the Vatican in Rome, where he had recently visited.

'From Thorfinn,' added Macbeth.

Lulach froze. Suddenly he knew exactly what the letter was about. 'His daughter?'

'She's thirteen,' said the King. 'High time she was married.'

Lulach put down the fish. He'd suddenly lost his appetite. He had always known this day was coming, though the King had never mentioned it again after their meeting with Thorfinn.

Suddenly he remembered his mother, all those years ago, sitting on the hill with the cows and talking about duty. She had been the same age as Thorfinn's daughter when she first married.

Did she love Father then? he thought suddenly. Or did she marry him from duty? For some reason that had never occurred to him before.

These days Queen Gruoch spent most of her time supervising Moray, acting as the mormaer she had never wanted to be. She was rarely able to spend time with the King and his tanist.

More duty, thought Lulach. Well, this is mine. He'd been waiting for this day since the handshake in the rain, all those years before. To help keep the land peaceful, to keep the alliance with Thorfinn safe.

'Will we be married at Scone?' he asked, as though unconcerned. 'Or in Moray?'

The King looked relieved. Perhaps he was expecting an argument, thought Lulach. 'Neither. Her father wishes her to be married from home. He doesn't want her sailing off till she's a married woman.' The King raised an eyebrow. 'It could be done by proxy, if you'd rather.'

Royalty were often married by proxy before they left home, with someone standing in for them at the ceremony.

Lulach shrugged. 'No, sire. I'll go myself.'

And meet Thorfinn the Raven Feeder once again, as well as his daughter. The dream of the blackened skull hardly came at all these days. But it was still hard to accept the idea of his father's killer as his father-in-law.

'Good.' The King gave a half smile. 'Thorfinn is easily offended.'

Thorfinn had recently declared himself independent of the Norwegian king — no longer the Norse earl of the Orkney Islands, but their king. Thorfinn had also fought alongside Macbeth's troops when King Duncan's son, Malcolm, had tried to seize the throne. Malcolm had been a child when Duncan had been killed. Now he was old enough to be king, and his English uncle was helping him. No, thought Lulach, you wouldn't want to get on the wrong side of Thorfinn.

'Thorfinn's been a good ally,' the King went on. 'And who knows when we'll need him again.'

Malcolm had been living down in England, at the court of the English king, Edward. Like other English kings, Edward believed that God had ordained that a king's son should become king after his father died — even if he were stupid or insane. King Edward was horrified at the very idea of electing a king. He was pleased to support a rebellion that would get rid of such dangerous ideas on his doorstep.

If Malcolm gained the throne he'd get rid of the elections too. He was half English, and had grown up there. What did he care for Alba's laws?

But Malcolm had failed. He'd fled back down south to England.

Lulach had been too young for that war. He was glad. And with Thorfinn as an ally, hopefully Scotland would be too strong for Malcolm ever to attack again, even with English help.

'I've heard a little about Thorfinn's daughter,' the King continued. 'Her name is Thora. They say she's beautiful.'

'Every earl's daughter is supposed to be beautiful,' returned Lulach, trying to keep his voice light. 'She's probably fat like her father.' With warts too, he thought gloomily.

'Perhaps she takes after her mother. Her mother died, you know, two years ago. Thorfinn has married again.'

The King threw a mutton bone to his favourite hound. The dog grabbed it and began to gnaw at it under the table.

The King laid his hand on Lulach's. 'If she's hideous you can leave her with your mother. Visit her once a year to breed your sons. They say she's fond of animals,' he added encouragingly, spearing a chunk of greasy eel with his knife. 'That shows she must have a good heart.'

Fond of animals? Lulach imagined Thorfinn's daughter watching her hawk rise from her wrist to pluck smaller birds from the sky and tear them into pieces. Or maybe she enjoyed bear baiting . . .

'I'd better head north soon,' he said casually. 'While the weather holds.'

The King relaxed slightly and nodded. They watched as one of the jugglers added the half-stripped sheep's head to his batons, and then a roast leg of mutton too, while the courtiers laughed and the dogs underneath the table drooled and hoped he'd drop it all.

Chapter 19

Lulach

So foul and fair a day I have not seen.
(*Macbeth*, Act I, Scene 3, line 38)

The ship was a trader working along the coast. This time she carried Lulach and his men instead of dried fish or bales of wool or furs or bolts of linen.

The sea winds blustered across the waves, sending them slapping against the boat. Seagulls circled the ship in hope of fish. Cormorants dived into the waves in its wake.

Lulach stared at the birds. He wondered what would happen if he played Kenneth's pipe to them. Would the cormorants call back?

The sails flapped and billowed up above. The wind played on the ship's taut ropes as if they were harp strings, sending them twanging. A sudden harder gust almost seemed to keel them over. Then the ship righted herself and plunged on through the waves.

The Captain laughed. 'Never fear, my Lord,' he yelled to Lulach over the wind and waves and sail's song. 'There's quite a gale today, but we've weathered worse!'

'Do you do this run often?' shouted Knut.

'Thorfinn's a good customer.' The captain's voice was hoarse from years of yelling above the wind. 'We take him wheat flour, oil, almonds, raisins, get dried fish and Greenland furs in exchange.'

'You know Thorfinn's household well?' asked Knut, too innocently.

The Captain nodded, rather than shout again.

'And his daughter?'

'Knut!' said Lulach sharply. Whatever the girl was like, she'd be his wife — maybe one day Queen of Alba. It wasn't right for any man — not even Knut — to gossip about her.

But the Captain just laughed. 'Oh, yes. The Lady Thora's well known.'

Well known for what? wondered Lulach. But there was no way he could ask the Captain. He caught Knut's eye and shook his head.

Besides, he thought, as the island came in view, a glimpse of deeper blue among sleet and the spray, I'll find out soon enough.

The 'never-silent', the great north wind, howled across the island. Sleet stung Lulach's cheeks as he stared at the pier. It was made of solid stone, with a shingle beach on either side.

The sleet made it hard to see, but as far as he could tell the island was deserted.

The Captain stroked his beard. 'Can't hear a thing except the wind. Shouldn't be quiet like this,' he said. 'Last time we were here you couldn't move for youngsters shouting and yelling. I don't like it. I don't like it at all.'

'Maybe there's sickness,' said Knut.

Lulach shook his head. '*Everyone* wouldn't be sick. There'd be people still about.' He turned to the Captain. 'Where's Thorfinn's house?'

The Captain pointed. 'Over there. You'd see it if it weren't for the sleet. It's a grand place. Store sheds enough for an army.'

Lulach considered. He wished Kenneth were here, or some other experienced soldier. But the King hadn't seen any reason to send Kenneth with a marriage party. Lulach would have to take charge himself.

'Knut, bring five of the men,' he said at last. 'No one else is to leave the ship. Keep her ready to sail with the tide,' he added to the Captain.

There was something wrong here. Very wrong.

The captain threw out the gangway. The seven of them bounded across it to the pier, the wind slashing at their faces. It seemed strange to feel solid land underfoot after two days rolling on the sea. I'd never make a sailor, thought Lulach, or a fisherman either.

Nothing moved. The land was silent. Only the wind screamed about them as they forced their bodies through the sleet.

'Lulach?'

'Yes?'

'The seagulls,' whispered Knut. 'Have you noticed?'

Lulach nodded. There were no gulls sheltering by the pier, waiting for fish guts. What could have happened for even gulls to desert the land?

They found the first body behind a clump of bushes by the road. It was a woman's. Her feet were bare and she wore no cloak — she must have fled in a hurry. Her throat had been cut from side to side and there was blood on her skirt too. A dog lay by her side, its wet fur slashed across the chest.

'It tried to save her,' said Knut quietly.

Lulach nodded. He felt sick. But if Knut, the ex-monk, could look at the woman's body without flinching, so could he.

'Should we bury her?' asked Knut.

'Not yet.'

Lulach sniffed. The wind smelled strange ... sweet, but stale as well. Almost like the chimney at home after it had been swept ...

Suddenly the curtain of sleet rose.

Lulach stared.

The hills were bare and charred. No trees, no bushes. A few walls showed grey against the darkened earth.

There was no long house, no store sheds. There was no sign of life at all.

Instead the land spread out black, flat and featureless, apart from a few lumps of blackened stone or timber.

And bodies. Not long dead, for they still had their shape — they weren't bloated. And their eyes hadn't yet been plucked by the ravens. Men's bodies, soldiers' bodies, with old scars on their arms to show the battles they'd survived before.

But this one had killed them.

Lulach walked among them, trying to stop the horror from showing on his face in front of the soldiers. It was like a nightmare, he thought. The howling wind, and numberless bodies tumbled on the ground. It was just like the nightmares after he had seen the blackened body of his father. Some of the bodies had been burned like his, twisted into strange shapes by the fire but still recognisable as human. Others were untouched, apart from the sword blows that had killed them, as though they had managed to escape from the flames only to meet death by steel instead.

But there were no women's bodies after the first one. No children's either. Whoever had done this had killed the men, but taken the women and children prisoner. They'd be in slave chains now. He wondered about the woman they had found. Had she almost escaped? Or fought, as they dragged her to the ships, and then they'd killed her?

And what of Thora, his bride? Had her bones been burned in this inferno? Or was she a slave in chains, on her way to her new master?

Who could have done this to a man as powerful as Thorfinn?

This was what his own land had been spared, he realised. Because of Macbeth's peace, Lulach had never had to face a battlefield of bodies, or households burned to bones.

He gestured to the guards. 'Spread out,' he ordered.

'What are we looking for?' asked Knut.

Lulach shrugged. 'Clues to who did this. Survivors. Anything you can find.' He looked at the charred ruins of Thorfinn's hall again. How could anyone have survived a fire like that?

His mind flashed back to his father's body. Was it some form of justice that Thorfinn had died in flames too?

No, thought Lulach. This wasn't war. These people were taken by surprise. And innocent people died here with Thorfinn. Including Thora.

He began to walk past the ruins, down towards the water, then noticed Knut was still with him. 'I don't need a guard,' he said shortly.

'Whoever did this might still be nearby.'

'We'd have heard them. Captives aren't quiet.'

He needed some time to himself, he thought suddenly. Time to make sure he showed none of the horror he felt to his men. Time to forget the smell of burned bodies, remembered from his childhood. Time to mourn Thora, a girl he hadn't even met. He hadn't wanted to marry her. But she didn't deserve this. It was all he could do for his bride now, to mourn her for a while.

Knut headed back to the ship. Lulach wandered down to the sea again. There was a beach, a small crescent of pebbles backed by smooth boulders, with thick black drifts of seaweed to show how far the tide had reached. The waves were comforting as they washed back and forth. Waves didn't care what happened to people. Their world went on, no matter what tragedy happened on land.

The salt wind lashed his face. No wonder the Norsemen cover their roofs with turf, thought Lulach. Otherwise the wind would blow them off. The shingle crunched underfoot.

And then he heard a noise.

Half roar, half scream, followed by mutterings and moans, then it began again.

Lulach stopped in shock. What on earth was it? Perhaps someone had survived the massacre back there. Someone so badly hurt they could only scream, over and over.

The noise continued, high and wild. Surely, thought Lulach, no human throat could make a sound like that!

He ran across the shingle in the direction of the sound and around a tiny headland. Then he stopped and stared.

The headland opened out onto a tiny beach, hidden from the shore, a semicircle of coarse white sand among the rocks. On the furthest rock sat a girl, her arms wrapped round herself in a vain attempt to stay warm. She was singing. But the noise he had heard hadn't come from her — her voice was lost in the sound coming from the creature next to her.

Suddenly the girl noticed him. She stopped singing and scrambled to her feet. A second later the creature gave a final hiss and mutter and was silent too.

Lulach stared. It was a seal. A half-grown seal. A whisper of superstitious fear ran through him. Was the girl a silkie, a seal woman, one of those who changed into human form on land, then turned back into a sea creature in the water? Who else would sing with a seal?

The girl gazed at him, poised as though to run. She was tall — nearly as tall as Lulach, although clearly a few years younger — and slim, with wet red hair falling in thick plaits to her waist. She wore a thick gold bracelet on one arm and her dress looked like fine linen. But it was torn and blackened, and there was a red burn mark across her face as well. Underneath the embroidered skirt her feet were bare and sandy, and blue with cold.

There was only one girl in the Orkneys he could think of who would wear clothes as fine as that.

'Thora?'

The girl stared at him. The seal stared too. Lulach wondered if seals ever attacked humans.

'Who are you?' Her voice was clear and firm, though Lulach could still see terror in her eyes and her lips trembled with the cold. She used Norse, but then repeated her words in Gaelic when he didn't respond. She spoke Gaelic well, with hardly a trace of accent.

'Lulach MacGillecomgain, Tanist to King Macbeth,' he said tentatively — and watched her tense body sag in relief.

He took off his cloak and held it out to her.

The girl took it, then stepped back again at once. She wrapped the cloak around herself, luxuriating in its warmth.

'Welcome to the Orkneys, Lulach MacGillecomgain,' she whispered through blue lips. She shut her eyes for a moment, as though to stop herself crying, then opened them again and stared at him. 'Though I'm afraid it's a poor welcome for a bridegroom.'

'What . . . what happened?' asked Lulach softly. He wanted to comfort her, to help her in some way. But she looked like she'd run if he came any nearer.

'Norse soldiers. Father had declared independence from the King of Norway, did you know?'

Lulach nodded. 'They attacked?'

'Three nights ago. It was midnight,' said Thora quietly. 'Father had posted guards about the Hall. But the soldiers didn't attack. Not then. They spilled whale oil about the Hall — I could smell it later — and then they tossed a torch.

'There was no time for our guards to fight. No time for anything. I heard Father yelling. It woke me up. He carried my stepmother through the flames . . .'

'And then he came back for you?'

'No,' said Thora flatly. 'I saved myself. The other women were screaming, running around in the light of the flames. It was easy for the King's soldiers to find them, to kill them, to . . . My nurse, my friends, the slaves . . . You know what men do to women in war, Lulach MacGillecomgain?'

'Yes,' said Lulach quietly.

'I ran into the dark. I kept on running to the sea. I heard someone behind me. I waited for a sword blow, or hands to grab me. But it was Father, with Ingeborg in his arms.'

'But why didn't the soldiers find you?' Lulach asked.

'The seals hid me,' said Thora simply. She stroked the seal's head. It gazed up at her adoringly. 'I asked them to hide Father and Ingeborg too. We crouched among them on the rocks, with the waves splashing about us. No one looked for us among the seals. And then . . . and then the soldiers sailed away. And we stayed here.'

Seals! Lulach stared at her. Maybe she really *was* a silkie! Why else would the seals obey her?

Suddenly Thora sat down again, on her rock. 'Have . . . have you any food, Lulach Mac Gillecomgain?' Her voice was steady, but Lulach could see the effort it took. 'Darling has been bringing us fish. But . . .' She tried to smile. 'Somehow raw fish doesn't fill me up like it does Darling.'

'Darling?'

Thora stroked the seal's smooth head. It gave a happy hiss. 'I raised her from a pup,' she said softly. 'She was an orphan. I've raised other seals too. They all went back to the sea. Seals remember. That's why the seals hid us. But Darling's still a baby. She sleeps on my bed.' Thora's voice trailed off, as though remembering that she had no bed any more.

'You mean Darling was with you that night? But how did she escape?' Lulach could have kicked himself. This was no time to question the poor girl.

But Thora smiled. 'I had to carry her.'

Lulach stared. She looked so vulnerable, sitting there in her wet dress with the fire scar on her cheek. But she had run through the flames when her father had chosen to save his new wife instead of his daughter. She had escaped the soldiers when every other woman had been caught. She had run through the darkness — and all this carrying a seal! And she had eaten raw fish to survive.

He wondered if there was another girl like this in all the world.

Lulach fumbled in his pouch. He usually kept sweetmeats there — dried apple, or cakes of oats and berries. He held one out to her. She came closer and took it, then stepped back and began to eat it hungrily.

'Where's your father?' Lulach asked quietly.

'Around the bay. Darling won't bring fish when he's near. I ... I sing to her. She likes singing. And then she brings the fish and I can share it with her and Father and Ingeborg.'

The men have probably found Thorfinn by now, thought Lulach. Or Thorfinn might have found *them*.

He hoped Thorfinn realised they were friends, not enemies, before anyone was hurt.

'You're safe now, Thora,' he said gently. 'No more raw fish. My ship's at the pier.'

Thora lifted her chin. 'I'm not going without Darling.'

The seal's big brown eyes stared at Lulach. Her whiskers twitched.

Lulach blinked. He'd heard ballads where heroes saved princesses. But they'd never had to save a seal as well. 'She can come too.'

'Are you sure? My father said ... he said that no king's heir would have a seal in his hall. I'd have to leave her behind. But I can't leave her. There's no one to look after her now. And she saved my life.'

'I promise,' said Lulach. 'Darling will be as welcome as you are. There's a river near our rath,' he added. 'And the sea's nearby. She'll be happy. I give you my word.'

Thora's eyes met his. 'My father said once, "Do you know what Macbeth's strongest weapon is? He tells the truth. Men trust him." That's why Scotland has peace, and England and Norway only war. So I'll trust you too, Lulach MacGillecomgain Macbeth.'

It was as though she had pinned a medal on his cloak. His heart felt strange, as though it had suddenly been filled. He'd never even known it was empty.

'Come on then,' he said gently.

Thora shook her head. 'She won't follow me with you here. You go first. We'll follow along the beach.'

Lulach hesitated. He didn't want to leave her, not alone on this desolate stretch of coast.

Suddenly Darling lifted her head again.

'*Carrraaaaggghhhhh!*' she bellowed.

Darling was singing again.

Her roar reached notes no human singer ever dreamed about: high one moment, low the next. Lulach wanted to put his hands over his ears.

'Sorry!' yelled Thora over the noise. 'She doesn't like being ignored!'

Suddenly Lulach had an idea. He pulled Kenneth's pipes from his pouch and began to play.

At the first note Darling stared at him and gave a startled hiss. And then — miraculously — the cove fell silent. There was just the music and the crashing of the waves, until the tune was finished.

Lulach put the pipes down. Darling had a faraway look. Her head still swayed with the memory of the music.

Thora stared at him. Suddenly she smiled. It was a faint smile, because her eyes were still tired and shadowed. But it was still a smile.

'She likes you,' said Thora softly. 'She'll follow you now, I think.'

Lulach grinned. He decided he liked Darling too.

Even better, he'd learned how to shut her up.

Chapter 20

Lulach

... the Norweyan banners flout the sky,
And fan our people cold ...
(*Macbeth*, Act I, Scene 2, lines 50–51)

Thorfinn was already on board when Lulach led Thora and Darling up the gangplank. The sailors stared at the seal as she bounced across the plank. Lulach glared at them and they swallowed their grins.

Thorfinn wore a blanket like a cloak and not much else. His bare legs were fat and hairy, and red in places with blisters from the fire. There was no sign of his wife. Knut must have taken her to the cabin below, thought Lulach.

'My Lord,' said Lulach politely, 'I'm sorry to see you in such a state.'

Thorfinn glanced at his daughter and then at the seal. Then he looked back at Lulach. 'I must thank you for our rescue,' he said uncomfortably.

Then his formality vanished. He met Lulach's eyes with a steady gaze. 'Just get me to the mainland, boy. I have supporters there. Give me six months and I'll rid the Orkneys of the Norwegian King's men. And my thieving nephew who helped him. In six months your father will have a worthwhile ally again.'

'My father will be glad you're safe, sir. And your wife and daughter.'

Thorfinn gave a grim laugh. 'Pretty words. No need to pretend, boy. The marriage is off. You've repaid any debt by rescuing us.'

Lulach looked at Thora, shivering next to him. Her father hadn't even spoken to her. And it had been his wife he'd rescued, not his daughter . . .

'On the contrary, sir,' said Lulach coldly. 'I wish to hold you to the betrothal. Thora shall come with me to Moray, to my mother. We will be married there — that's if . . .' he hesitated, 'if the Lady Thora still wishes it.'

Thorfinn gave his barking laugh again. 'You'd take a penniless girl? And her forsaken seal! You're a fool, boy.'

'Then when I'm king they can call me Lulach the Fool,' said Lulach calmly. He turned to the shivering girl. 'Thora?'

Everyone was listening. But Lulach found he didn't care. Kings and princes had no privacy anyway. They may as well all listen now.

'I come to this marriage willingly,' he went on. 'But if you don't wish it, tell me. You'll still be my mother's guest at Moray, for as long as you want.'

Suddenly Darling lolloped across the deck to Lulach. She stared up at him and gave a sharp bark, then butted his knees. Thora was grinning at him. For a moment Lulach saw a glimpse of the girl she could be.

'Darling wants you to play again,' she said.

Lulach took her hand impulsively. She looked surprised, but didn't pull it away.

'I can promise you peace,' he said sincerely. 'My father is a king of peace. And I will be too, if they elect me when he's dead.'

'Good,' said Thora simply, her hand still in his. 'And, yes, Lulach MacGillecomgain, I *would* like to be your bride.'

Chapter 21

Luke

... and every one did bear
Thy praises ...

(*Macbeth*, Act I, Scene 3, lines 98–99)

Luke woke as the alarm clock shrilled by his bed. He rolled over to turn it off and smiled. He felt good. It had been an awesome dream.

So, thought Luke, *that* was how the story ended. A land of peace and plenty, despite Thorfinn's wars up north and Malcolm brooding down south. Macbeth loved by his subjects. Lulach happy, married to Thora.

Luke wondered if he'd managed to keep Darling off the bed.

Of course, there had to be more to it than that. Macbeth had died, Lulach had died. But it was all a thousand years ago.

He smiled to himself.

What did it matter now? They'd lived and been happy. Mrs Easson was right. It was a long time ago, far in the past even when Shakespeare had written his play. What did it matter if the Macbeth that people remembered now wasn't the real one? Maybe his name wouldn't have been remembered at all if it hadn't been for Shakespeare.

No, thought Luke. Too much truth could hurt. Sometimes it was better to bury the truth.

Dimly he remembered Thorfinn's voice — the hoarse, too-loud voice of a man used to shouting in battle or above the fierce north wind — and Thora quoting him: 'Do you know what Macbeth's strongest weapon is? He tells the truth.'

No, thought Luke. Too much truth could hurt.

He'd do his assignment tonight, just the way Mrs Easson expected him to, showing how Shakespeare's Macbeth had gone from being a weak but loyal man to a villain. And everything else would work out somehow. He'd keep quiet about the exam, and hopefully the Fishers would be okay.

At least if they had to sell out he wouldn't be here to see it. He'd be at St Ilf's.

Maybe he'd meet a girl like Thora for himself down in Sydney. But all he could think of was Megan, the bright flash of her hair as she pruned the trees . . .

Chapter 22

Luke

Son: And must they all be hang'd who swear
and lie?
Lady Macduff: Every one.
(*Macbeth*, Act IV, Scene 2, lines 51–52)

For once school was okay. It was almost as though real life had decided to follow Luke's dream. He even got every answer in his Maths test.

Maybe Mum and Sam were right, he thought happily, climbing onto the bus that afternoon. Maybe the only reason he had done so badly at school was because he'd missed all that time when Dad was sick. Maybe he *would* be able to cope at St Ilf's, even if he hadn't really won the scholarship . . .

Patrick and Megan were waiting for him at the back of the bus.

He was almost tempted to say, '*How now, you secret, black, and midnight hag!*' to Meg. Somehow that line from the play had stuck in his head. But she mightn't think it was funny.

'Hi,' he said instead.

'Hi, yourself,' said Megan, moving up the back seat to give him room to sit down. 'Hey, are you going to the meeting down at the hall tonight? For people who want to protest against the development?'

'Yeah, Mum told me she was organising it with your mum. They haven't given people much notice, have they? Mum was still ringing people up last night.'

'No choice,' said Megan. 'The Council meeting is next week.'

Luke watched her as she gazed out the window. Normally Megan would be yakking away like the rest of the kids on the bus. He'd never seen her so quiet before.

He hadn't thought it would affect her so much. She'd always been bored by the work on the farm. Pat was the one he discussed cattle breeds with, who planned to go to Ag college and talked of farming as though he'd never thought of anything else to do when he left school.

Luke got off at his usual stop, before Meg and Pat, and began the walk up to the house. He could hear Mum down in the bottom paddock as he trudged up the drive.

'*And though my love lies bleedin', I know she'll hear my cry, "Just bury me ... in Texas ... when ... I ... die!"*'

Luke grinned. He wondered what the cows thought of Mum's singing. They must be used to it by now.

Suddenly he didn't want to go inside. It'd been such a great day and he wasn't ready to go indoors yet.

He could go down and help Mum and Mr T tag the weaners. But they didn't really need him. And anyway, he felt like being alone.

Luke dumped his school bag by the garage and headed back across the paddocks, then up the hill into the rough country again. It was as though he could really breathe up here.

There was a flat rock platform at the top, five metres long at least and almost as wide, just past their boundary with the Fishers' place. This was where he and Pat and Megan had played Explorers when they were small, or pretended they were bushrangers trying to see the troopers far below. But it had been ages since Luke had climbed up here.

He headed for the rock now, then clambered up and sat on the edge, feeling the warmth seep into his body. He could see his place from here, and the Fishers' too, and the orchards and Mum's cows. He could even see Mr Fisher, small as a Lego man in the cabin of his tractor as he sprayed a white cloud on the trees. Fungicide, thought Luke vaguely. Curly leaf, brown rot ...

No, he wouldn't want to have an orchard again. Japanese Wagyu, yeah, that was the way to go, with really good feed ...

'Luke!'

Luke jumped, then turned round. Megan was staring at him from below the rock. 'What are you doing here?' he asked.

'I live here,' said Megan. 'Remember?'

'Oh. Yeah,' said Luke, embarrassed. He'd forgotten it was the Fishers' land. 'Sorry. I just came up here to ...' He tried to think of something that didn't sound dumb, but all he could come up with was, 'to think.'

'Really?' Megan held out her hand. For a moment he didn't understand, then worked out she wanted a hand up. 'I come up here too sometimes,' she added, sitting down next to him.

It was no closer than they'd sat on the bus. But for some reason it *seemed* closer. He could even feel her warmth.

Neither of them said anything for a while. Why do I feel so nervous around Megan all of a sudden? thought Luke. What had changed between them?

'What do you think about?' asked Megan suddenly.

Luke shrugged. 'Not sure. Things.' It sounded so lame he felt himself flushing.

But Megan didn't seem to notice how lame it was. She wasn't even looking at him, but at the farms below.

'This is going to be my place, after Dad dies,' she said.

'You mean, really yours? He's leaving it to you?'

'Just this bit, the forty hectares up the mountain. The rest goes to Patrick.'

'You don't mind?' It'd be like a sword thrust into him if Mum left the farm to anyone else, Luke realised.

'Not really. Makes sense. Pat's always wanted to be a farmer. I don't. But I want to live here.'

'What do you want to do, then?' he asked cautiously.

'Study law.'

'You mean, to fight developers like the resort people?'

Megan laughed. 'That too, maybe. No, wills, contracts for houses. The day-to-day stuff that people round here need help with. It'd mean I could still live here and make a living without having to prune trees when it's freezing, or get covered in peach fuzz every summer, or stare at cows' bums.'

'I don't mind cows' bums,' said Luke. He was surprised to find how much he meant it. Farming — what else would he ever want to do?

Did they even have an Ag course down at St Ilf's?

'Okay, a few cows to look decorative,' said Megan. 'Even some fruit trees, maybe. But I want to do something else as well.'

'You can still build your house here, even if the resort goes ahead,' said Luke.

'Not if Dad has to sell the farm.'

Luke stared. 'He can't! I mean, I thought he'd just have to do something else. But you'd still live here.'

'What job could he do around here? I don't think we could afford to keep the place.' Megan shrugged. 'Dad and Mum haven't said anything. But I know that's what they're thinking.'

'I . . . I can't imagine this place without you and Pat.'

Megan's face seemed to crumple for a moment, then she was back in control. 'The farm's important. It's . . . it's not just that it's how Dad makes a living. It was his pa who planted the first peaches. His great-something grandmother — I can't remember how many back — was the first white kid born around here.'

'I didn't know that.'

'People talk about how Aboriginal people are close to their land,' said Megan vehemently. 'And they are. But we've been here for a hundred and seventy years. It'd kill Dad to have to stop farming here. Pat too. I don't mean they'd actually die — they just wouldn't be, well, who they really are.' Suddenly she looked over at Luke. 'Things like this are too precious to be lost. Someone has to fight for them.'

'Yeah.' Suddenly Luke's memory thrust up Mum saying, 'Sometimes you have to fight.'

But that hadn't been Mum, Luke remembered. It had been Lulach's mother, Gruoch, Lady Macbeth. And she hadn't been talking about saving the land, but about Alba, ancient Scotland.

Is there anything I'd fight for? he wondered. Really fight? He had never thought of it before. Maybe you only found out how much things meant to you when they were threatened . . . Sam *had* to help the Fishers, he thought.

'And that's what you want to say? On TV?'

Megan nodded. 'Some things are important,' she said. 'But people don't realise they are till you tell them.'

Suddenly Luke thought of Thora in his dream. She'd had guts too. But he couldn't see Megan running from the flames, a seal in her arms. She'd have been in the middle of everything, sword whirling in her hand . . .

Megan would be good on TV, thought Luke. She'd convince people. If only he had her courage. Or Thora's.

'I'll . . . I'll ask Sam again,' he said. And he would, he thought. No matter what Sam said, this time he wasn't going to chicken out.

Even if it wouldn't be any use.

'Thanks,' said Megan simply. She was crying, Luke realised. There were tears in her eyes. But she didn't wipe them away, or make any kind of sound.

He wished he could hug her, or comfort her in some way. Then suddenly it didn't matter. She had burrowed her head into his shoulder and was crying properly. He put his arm around her and felt her warmth again, the softness of her hair.

Suddenly she pulled away and sniffed. 'Sorry,' she said.

'It's okay,' said Luke gently. He knew he should say something comforting. But he couldn't think what to say.

'It's just that everything is going wrong!' choked Megan. 'The farm threatened, and you going off to Sydney . . .' Her voice trailed off, as though she had just noticed what she'd said.

'I'd better go,' she added hurriedly. 'Mum'll wonder where I am. Will you be at the meeting tonight?'

'Of course,' said Luke. 'Meg . . .'

'Mmm?' Megan was blowing her nose.

'Would you like to — I mean — how about going to the movies or something this Saturday?'

Megan looked at him, surprised. 'You mean without Patrick? Just you and me?'

Luke nodded.

Suddenly a new look slid over Megan's face. It was happiness, thought Luke, astounded. She really looked happy! But all she said was, 'Okay.'

She slid off the rock and began to run back down the hill.

Chapter 23

Luke

Is this a dagger, which I see before me,
The handle toward my hand?

(*Macbeth*, Act II, Scene 1, lines 33–34)

It was impossible to walk straight home. Not after all that. Luke wandered back to the top paddock and leaned over the gate, watching the cows. Cows were good to watch when your brain was in turmoil, he decided. Cows were restful things most of the time, just standing there eating.

Did Megan really like him? More than she liked Jingo?

How could he make Sam see how important the Fishers were? People like them shouldn't be forced from the place they loved just because tourists wanted golf courses and spas.

It was hard to know what to think about, or what to feel ... but finally he noticed how the shadows were lengthening behind the cows. He jogged down the rest of the hill, avoiding the cowpats from long practice.

Mum was back from the bottom paddock when he reached home. He could hear her in the kitchen as he came through the front door, out of tune again.

'*Country ho ... me, Take me* — oh, blast! I dropped it — *hooo ... ooooome* ... Luke, is that you? I've been wondering when you'd get home. Where have you been?'

'Went for a walk,' said Luke.

There was a cake on the table. One of Mum's, thought Luke. Which meant it was edible. He grabbed a knife and cut into it. Chocolate. The icing was still soft, but it was good.

'I hope you didn't forget about the meeting tonight,' said Mum. She was wearing a dress with a soft draped front, a new one she must have bought down in Sydney last weekend. 'You'd better get changed. We've just got time to get down there. We can have dinner later.'

'Sure,' said Luke. 'You've still got your boots on,' he added with a grin.

'Have I?' Mum looked down. 'Damn. So I have.' She vanished out the door to the new wing. 'Don't eat all the cake!' her voice floated back to him. 'I want to take it down to the meeting in case people want a cuppa later.'

It was strange driving down the shadowed road to town with Mum. Almost like old times, when they'd drive down every night in the old truck, after a quick dinner, to see Dad at the hospital, in those last weeks when he could no longer be looked after at home.

The time before Sam.

He'd finally tried to call Sam before they left. But there was just Sam's voice on the machine in his apartment. 'Hi, this is Sam Mackenzie. I'm not here at the moment, but leave a message after the beep . . .'

He'd called Sam's mobile too, but it was turned off. What could Sam be doing? Luke wondered in frustration. His mobile was always off when he was filming, but surely filming was over for the day.

He tried to think what he'd say to Sam. 'You owe me,' he'd tell him. 'You made me a cheat.'

Except he didn't, Luke admitted to himself. I made *myself* a cheat. I could've put my hand up at any time and said, 'Hey, I've seen this paper before.' And then I wouldn't be going to St Ilf's next year . . .

In spite of everything, a smile slid over his face. Was Megan really upset about him going to St Ilf's? She'd seemed happy he'd got the scholarship. Maybe she was happy for him, and sad for herself.

His smile grew bigger as they drew up outside the hall, at the thought of seeing her again.

The Breakfast Creek Town Hall had been built in the 1930s when the town was just a handful of houses, a couple of churches, a pub and a school for the children from the farms around. As the land along the coast filled up with holiday homes and retirees, and the town grew larger, a new hall had been built. Now this one was kept for anyone who wanted to hire it for a day or an evening. The local scouts and the quilters used it and the school held its annual play there.

This evening the fibro walls had a *Save Our Water!* poster stickytaped by the door. There were only two other cars in the car park.

Mum looked at her watch. 'It's still early,' she said hopefully. 'The meeting's not supposed to start till six.'

'Yeah.' Luke got out of the car and went inside.

The lights were on. The Fishers were up the front by the stage, with Mrs Robinson and her son, who lived further up the valley. They'd already put out about fifty chairs. Somehow the hall looked even emptier with the empty chairs.

'Hi!' Mum greeted them, a bit too brightly. She put the sliced chocolate cake down by the tea urn, which was bubbling on a table at the back. There was already a plate of pikelets there, spread with butter and plum jam, and an orange cake.

Luke wandered down and sat next to Patrick and Megan. 'Hi,' he said. He was glad Pat was there too. He felt a bit embarrassed meeting Megan after this afternoon. Had she told Pat she'd seen him? Or that he'd asked her out?

'Hi,' said Patrick. There didn't seem to be any more they could say. They sat in silence for a while. Mum and the Fishers and Mrs Robinson were chatting about sending more letters to the paper.

A car pulled up outside. Luke turned as Mr Donnelly from the local paper stuck his head in, camera in hand, then saw the empty hall. 'Might come back later!' he called as he went back out again.

They waited a bit longer. Luke looked at his watch. Six-fifteen.

Megan's face was white. 'No one's coming, are they?' she whispered. 'They just don't care!'

Mum had overheard. 'It was late notice,' she said. 'We only put the posters up two days ago. Maybe we should have advertised a speaker ...' Her voice trailed away.

'Sometimes people need to be told what to care about,' said Megan softly. 'They just don't realise what's at stake till it's too late.'

Sam should have been here, thought Luke. People would have come if they'd thought Sam was going to speak.

The unspoken words hovered in the silent hall.

The drive home was quiet. There were just too many words they couldn't say.

Luke wanted to rage at Mum. Yell at her. Why don't *you* get Sam to do something?

But Mum had been through too much. Sam made her happy. Sam looked after her. Sam the TV host and Mum the scruffy farmer's widow. No, whatever happened between Mum and Sam, Luke knew there was a big sign saying 'Keep Out!' There had just been too many years when he'd longed to be able to do something that would make Mum really happy . . .

'Hey, Sam's home!' said Luke in surprise as they drove up the driveway. The courtyard lights were on and Sam's four-wheel drive was parked outside the big new double garage. The garage doors were shut, though they'd been open when he and Mum left.

He didn't know whether to be sorry or relieved. It would be easier to ask Sam about the Fishers again in person. But he hadn't expected to have to do it so soon.

'Open the garage door, will you, Luke?' asked Mum. They were the first words she'd spoken since they left the Fishers at the hall.

Luke opened the ute door as Sam came out of the house. 'Hi, mate!' he said cheerily, as though the argument before he left had never happened. 'Got a surprise for you!'

'For me?' asked Luke warily. Sam kissed Mum through the ute window. 'Sure,' he said, giving the wide, practised smile that viewers saw six days a week. 'I came up this afternoon,' he added to Mum. 'Picked it up on my way home.'

'What is it?' Isn't he going to ask where we've been? thought Luke, as Mum got out of the ute. But maybe she told him about the meeting this afternoon on the phone.

He could have been there, thought Luke. He hasn't even asked us how it went . . .

'How did the meeting go?' asked Sam.

'It didn't,' said Luke shortly. 'No one turned up.'

'I'm sorry to hear that,' said Sam — giving his concerned look, thought Luke. Sam smiled, and pressed the control for the garage doors.

They opened.

Luke stared.

In the middle of the garage was a four-wheeled motorbike, shiny red, with big balloon tyres.

'. . . so they don't cut into the grass,' Sam was saying. He grinned at Luke, the confident grin familiar to TV watchers all over Australia. But his eyes were strangely anxious. 'Do you like it?'

'Of course he likes it!' said Mum quickly.

'Luke?' Sam had lost his smile.

Luke looked at Sam, and then back at Mum. He looked at the bike. Then he looked at Sam again.

He knew that Sam knew what he was thinking. Do you think that you can buy my silence? Make me like you — someone who lies for what he wants, pretends he's concerned every day on TV but really does nothing, nothing . . .

'Luke?' Mum's voice was uncertain now.

Luke hesitated. But why say the words? Sam knew them. He was sure that Sam knew them.

Luke forced a smile. 'It's wonderful. Thanks heaps!' He hugged Mum briefly, looking at Sam over her shoulder. And suddenly he knew that there *was* something he could do for Mum.

'Aren't you going to try it out?' asked Mum. 'Sam thought, well, you're always over at the Fishers' and it's a long way. On the bike you can be there and back in a jiffy. What's that song . . .'

'"The Motorbike Song",' said Luke. It was one of Mum's favourites. 'Sure, I'll give it a buzz.'

Two wheelies, he thought, and once down the track into the darkness. Then I can go to my room . . .

. . . and not cry till I get there.

He didn't know why the tears were there. But he did know that he'd rather crash the bike than allow them to be seen.

Chapter 24

Luke

I have no words;
My voice is in my sword . . .
(*Macbeth*, Act V, Scene 8, lines 6–7)

'Luke?'

Luke looked up from his homework.

It was Mum. She slipped inside the door. She'd taken off the dress she'd worn to the meeting and put on her old jeans with the cow stains again.

She sat down on his bed. 'I just wanted to thank you,' she said.

Luke stared. 'What for?'

Mum smiled. It was a strange smile. An almost adult-to-adult smile. 'You know. About the bike.'

'What about it?'

'I know you couldn't care less about it. But you pretended. You thanked him.'

Luke shrugged. There was too much he wanted to say. Why didn't *you* make him help the Fishers? How can you love a man like that after Dad?

'I know it must be hard for you to accept Sam

sometimes. But it's ... it's not easy for Sam either, you know,' said Mum finally.

'What!' Luke stared. 'Why not?'

'Lots of reasons. His work. There's always someone younger, tougher, wanting to take over. And Sam knows it. He knows that any day someone might axe the show. Or keep the show and get another presenter.'

'He'd get another job, though, wouldn't he?'

'Maybe. But there aren't all that many current affairs shows ...'

'What does that matter?' muttered Luke.

'It matters to Sam.'

'Why? He's rich enough now, isn't he? He just likes everyone thinking he's so great. But he's not really the man they see on TV at all.'

'You're right in a way,' said Mum. 'The real Sam's more complex than the public one. Sam seems confident. But he isn't.' Mum hesitated. 'Sometimes I think he needs to see his face on the screen to know who he is. He's a good man, Luke. Really. He does care about things. Even if you can't see it sometimes.'

'But you can?'

'Yes,' said Mum. 'I can.'

Suddenly Mum looked awkward. 'It's not easy for him here sometimes either,' she added. 'A ... a stepson's a big thing to take on. He does his best, Luke. Even if ... even if you don't think it's a very good best sometimes. He really does care about you.'

She hesitated again. 'He told me once that we're the rock he comes back to every weekend. Real life. You and me, this place. He needs us more than you realise.'

Luke was silent for a moment. Sam needed them? It was all so different from what he'd imagined. Could Mum possibly be right? Would she still feel the same about Sam — or Luke — if she knew about the exam?

'Mum . . . are you happy? With Sam, I mean.'

Mum looked surprised. 'Of course.' Suddenly she gave that adult smile again. 'I've got all I ever wanted, Luke. But Sam has to keep fighting for it. Every day.'

I don't need to know this, thought Luke.

Or did he?

He was still wondering when Mum left the room.

Chapter 25

Luke and Lulach

Fair is foul, and foul is fair:
Hover through the fog and filthy air.
(*Macbeth*, Act I, Scene 1, lines 11–12)

Luke decided he wasn't going to think about what Mum had said now. He'd finish his homework then think about it tomorrow.

Maybe.

He looked back down at the notes on his desk. For the past couple of hours he'd been trying to write his talk on *Macbeth* on the computer. Tomorrow was Friday, and he'd spent so long trying to work out what to say that he hadn't even started it till tonight.

But it was just what Mrs Easson wanted. He'd shown how Macbeth was tricked by the witches into killing King Duncan because they'd told him he was going to be king instead; how a loyal man became a murderer, then had to kill more people just to be safe ...

All he had to do now was read it out tomorrow. It was finished. Done.

He pressed *Print*, and waited while the pages floated out beside him.

Who cared if it didn't really happen like that? What was one more lie?

He'd been trapped, just like Macbeth in the play. Trapped into pretending about the bike, trapped into cheating, trapped into going to St Ilf's. Trapped into lying to Megan about Sam as well.

What did it matter if he added one more lie to the pile, and lied about what an evil king Macbeth had been too, so he'd get a good mark?

Time for sleep. At least the dream might come again, thought Luke, as he got ready for bed. Lulach happy married to Thora; Macbeth ruling a peaceful land.

Luke lay down and reached over to turn off the light.

Once again the dream came swiftly, as though the past had sucked him in. One moment he was a kid, falling asleep in his bed, and the next . . .

He was in a tent. Someone was practising a drumbeat outside. And all around were the sounds of an army at night-time: some sleeping, others sleepless as they prepared for war . . .

No! thought Luke. It shouldn't be like this! This was supposed to be a good dream! Not a dream about war!

But neither Lulach nor Luke could escape.

It was late summer, the heather flowering on the hills. Winters were too cold for war: the snow too deep, the winds too harsh. And there wasn't enough food in spring to feed an army. But in late summer, as the fields grew rich with harvest, the battlefields grew ripe with war.

Tomorrow would be the Feast of the Seven Sleepers back home in Moray. But no one feasted here.

Lulach lay in his tent and waited. It was a sturdy tent, as befitted the King's tanist. He was lucky; most of the men slept with nothing but their cloaks to keep away the cold.

Lulach had tried to sleep. Sleep had always been a refuge, ever since he was small. But not tonight. Sleep refused to come.

Beyond the tent he could hear snores, grunts, whispers — all the noises of sleeping men. At least he had privacy in these last hours.

It was the waiting that was the worst, he thought — then snorted. How could he know what was the worst thing in a battle? He'd never taken part in one.

Almost to the last he had hoped that his stepfather would work out some trick — an alliance, perhaps, or an ambush, as he had all those years before when Thorfinn's men attacked. But this was war, not a cattle raid.

Malcolm, Duncan's son, had ridden north again, with soldiers from the English king and the army of his uncle, the Earl of Northumbria. Malcolm, who cared nothing for Alba's laws, who only wanted power, any way that he could grab it.

The army of Alba had tramped down south. Now the two armies camped at each end of a wide glen, near enough to see the smoke from each other's fires. But the enemy had far more fires than theirs. The English army was three times the size of Alba's.

When the sun rose, each army would line up, facing each other. And then they'd charge. And then . . .

And then?

Something moved outside his tent. A voice said softly, 'Lulach?'

Knut.

'I'm awake,' called Lulach.

His friend opened the tent flap and stepped in. Outside, the grey night sky above the glen was beginning to turn pink. Lulach could even make out the hills around them and the occasional grove of trees. A world of shadows, after the peace of night.

'Couldn't you sleep either?' asked Lulach.

Knut shrugged. He pushed Lulach's spare cloak off the chest that held his armour, and sat down. Lulach passed him his water bag. It was filled with Thora's heather ale, the taste of home. Knut took a mouthful, then nodded his thanks.

'I've got some bread and cheese,' offered Lulach.

'I'm not hungry.'

They sat in silence. What did you say just before your first battle?

Finally Lulach said lightly, 'You could have been safe in your abbey this morning if you hadn't become my equerry.'

Knut looked surprised, as though he had never thought that fate would lead him anywhere but here. 'What do you mean? We have to fight.'

Fighting for a just cause doesn't mean you wouldn't rather be somewhere else, thought Lulach. If he were honest, he'd say he would rather be back at the Hall with Thora and his mother, helping with the harvest. Anywhere, anything but this. But he said nothing.

'When this is over,' said Knut softly, 'I'm going to ask the King to release me from his service.'

'Not back to your abbey?'

Knut smiled. 'No. I'm not meant to be a monk. But I've had enough of being an equerry too. Even yours. There's a girl, Kenneth's granddaughter, Alianna. Do you know her?'

Vaguely, thought Lulach. Short girl, dark hair. He nodded.

'I'll have had my share of glory when this is over,' said Knut lightly. 'I want to marry, watch cattle on the hill, raid my neighbour's herd when I get bored.'

I wish I could do the same, thought Lulach. But he just smiled.

'Do you think the King's plan will work?' asked Knut at last.

'Of course,' said Lulach automatically.

Would it work? he wondered. It was their only chance.

The camp was stirring now, men calling to each other. Lulach and Knut went outside.

Mist hung over the hills like a linen tablecloth. Somewhere above the mist it was summer. But this morning, summer seemed as far away as peace.

Misty light began to invade the camp. Men put their armour on — the few who had any. Boys ran about, shouting with excitement at the prospect of their first battle. Horsemen polished their double-edged, sharp-pointed claymores, and foot soldiers cleaned their daggers on the spikes of their shields.

The men lined up, ready for battle. There were jokes, insults for the English in general and Malcolm's men in particular, boasts about the number of enemies each man would handle. There are three English soldiers for every one of ours, thought Lulach. Do we have a hope of winning?

He glanced at the King, joking with one of his men. Macbeth planned to use strategy instead of might today, just as he had so long ago when he burned the boats of Thorfinn's men.

Would it be enough?

Macbeth mounted his horse — an old one, steady, but with sufficient stamina to last the day. Lulach rode on his right-hand side, Kenneth on his left.

'Men of Alba!' The King's words echoed across the valley. Suddenly the army was silent. 'We are fighting for our homes, our loved ones! This land gave us our lives. Now we give it back our hearts and blood. What is a man if he can't fight for what he loves? And whenever each of you faces the enemy today, say, as I will do: "My feet are on my native soil! I strike this blow for Alba!"'

'For Alba! For Macbeth!' The cheers were so loud Lulach was sure the English army must hear them.

Someone yelled, 'And bum cheese to the English!' Laughter mingled with the cheers. The men waved their claymores joyfully in the air.

What are we really fighting for? wondered Lulach. Why is it so important to have one king rather than another? Macbeth was a good king, yes, but it was more than that.

Law, he thought. We're really fighting for Alba's law. Our right to elect our king instead of have an invader make himself king by force. But how many men would cheer if I called out, 'We are fighting for our laws!'

It's strange, he thought, looking at the men and boys around him. It's almost as though these men are going to a feast, they seem so eager to engage the enemy.

But not him. Nor, he thought, the King. If Macbeth had enjoyed war the country wouldn't have had so many years of peace.

The army began to march up the nearest hill into the mist: one long straight row of foot soldiers, with the King and his guards and the other horsemen behind. The rocks threw shadows on either side, crouching like misshapen sheep in the first of the morning light.

The white air clung to Lulach's skin, but below them it was clear. He could see the English army down in the glen. So many, he thought. The English had hired men from Ireland too. Malcolm not only had more troops — he had more horsemen too. A man on horseback could kill a hundred foot soldiers. Please, thought Lulach, let the King's plan work.

The mist rose suddenly, like a sheet pulled off a bed. Now the sky was a soft blue. Too gentle for a battle, thought Lulach. War should be fought on stormy days.

The English army could see them now too. They began to line up in their usual 'war hedge', three rows deep. The first row of soldiers carried shields and spears in front of them. They wore strange helmets, leather caps that covered their noses as well as their hair, so that they looked like a line of brown-headed beasts.

The second row was swordsmen, with more rows of swordsmen behind. The enemy horsemen were assembled on either side.

A piper's first doubtful notes floated up from the glen, and then the full skirl of the pipes.

The enemy began to march up the hill towards the army of Alba.

The King raised his voice, though not enough for the English to hear. 'Wait till they are halfway up the hill! No one move until you see the signal. Remember the plan!'

It was a good plan, thought Lulach. Force the English to come up the hill towards them. They'd be puffed, and it was hard to send spears uphill. Much easier to slash at an enemy below you.

Yes, it was a good plan. But would it work?

Lulach could hear the English drumbeat under the piper's song. *Battered a, battered a, battered a tent, battered a tent, battered a tent . . .*

It suddenly occurred to him that this might be the day he'd die.

'You'll be right, lad,' called Kenneth, as if he could read his thoughts. Beside him Knut fingered the hilt of his claymore.

Steadily, almost silently, apart from the pipes and drumbeat, the English climbed up the hill. Their horses skittered at its steepness. The soldiers were already panting in their armour.

Closer . . . closer . . .

Lulach could see their faces now beneath their helmets, hear the beat of their feet . . .

'Start the chant,' ordered the King.

Kenneth began it, then Lulach and Knut joined in. The sound ran down the Scottish lines.

'Out! Out! Out! Out!'

Out of our country, thought Lulach. Out of our lives.

'Out! Out! Out!'

The King punched the air, the signal that meant 'Charge!'

The Alban foot soldiers began to run, each man holding his shield with its sharp point in front, his claymore high, his dirk behind his sword. Each man screamed defiance at the enemy.

Suddenly a hail of spears flew up from the English lines. But most went wide or failed to reach the Albans. The rest fell harmlessly against their shields. The English soldiers weren't used to sending spears uphill.

'Out! Out! Out! Out!'

Suddenly a hail of rocks rained down on the English. The army of Alba might not have as many spears as the English, but rocks were free, and easily thrown downhill.

You couldn't hear the enemy piper now, only the yells of the Alban army. The rain of rocks was finished. Down, down, down the foot soldiers ran . . .

Lulach pulled at his reins, as his horse tried to join in the charge. 'Steady,' he whispered, as much to himself as the horse.

Could they really win? It seemed impossible, so few against so many.

All at once the armies met, the flying Highlanders surging down the slope into the English troops, who were labouring uphill. Lulach watched as the first English line went down, skewered by the points on the Alban shields.

And then the second line collapsed, bludgeoned by the claymores, which swept down onto their necks, their shoulders.

Two lines gone ... then screams, as the Highland daggers met the third line of English soldiers.

For a moment the black image of his father's body flashed into Lulach's mind. This was what war meant. Agony. Death.

Then the image was gone, as the excitement of the charge captured Lulach too.

The big English horses were stumbling on either side, unable to find their footing.

The King yelled, 'Now!' The Alban horsemen charged, the stocky Highland ponies sure of foot. Their riders screamed the challenge, their swords whirling above them and onto the horsemen below.

Lulach yelled with the others. Fear had vanished. This was how to outride, outfight, an English army. The enemy troops scattered into chaos.

But even chaos needed to be fought.

The world changed. A moment before, Lulach had seen the whole glen, the hills around. He had been conscious of the wider world as well: the enemy England; the land of Alba, safe for now under its rule of law.

Now the world narrowed. All he knew was the weight of his claymore, the strength of his shoulders as he twirled it high above his head. He had trained for this with Kenneth ever since he was a lad. Now it almost seemed as though the sword moved by itself.

Slash down on one side, then the other. A man on horseback has the power of a hundred men on foot.

Slash, and slash again ...

How can you explain your first battle? Even if you've grown up in a land where most men have been to war, you can never understand it until you've fought in a battle yourself.

Slash, and slash ... exhilaration grows with every enemy you kill. Each enemy down means one more moment you've survived.

But which are the enemy? The English wear their leather caps but it is still difficult to tell one man from another in the confusion. You give the battle cry again, and hear the men around you echo it, so you know that they at least are yours.

Slash, and slash ... Impossible to yell the battle cry again. Breath is too precious to waste on a yell. Most of the English horses have been driven back. But there are still a few who've manoeuvred through the Alban ranks, their riders slashing at the foot soldiers below.

The smell of blood, of metal as swords clash ...

Screams of agony — so many that after a while they are just one scream from a thousand mouths, till suddenly your horse steps back onto a dying man ...

Clash, parry, clash ... You fight the man in front, always fearing the man behind. That's why you fight back to back with someone you trust ...

Knut, heaving at his sword, was panting behind Lulach. Was this what they had dreamed of all those years ago, as Kenneth showed them how to wield a broadsword?

Suddenly another English horseman struck Lulach from the side. Lulach felt the blow on his left shoulder, saw the enemy lift his sword again ...

And suddenly the horseman vanished. The King's horse was next to him, the King's shield protected him. Then it was gone, no longer needed. Lulach turned to meet another foe.

'*I will not yield, To kiss the ground before young Malcolm's feet . . .*'

Who said that? thought Lulach vaguely. Was it the King?

Clash, parry, clash . . .

'*And damn'd be him that first cries, "Hold, enough!"*'

Clash, parry . . .

So much noise! thought Luke, half waking a thousand years away. How can I sleep?

But he didn't want to sleep. Not if sleep meant he had to live through this. It's not fair! he thought. It's bad enough that things like this happened once, without bringing them back to life! Let the battle go! Please, let it pass!

And then it did.

The dream sucked at him once again. But now the battle was over.

He had survived.

Across the glen Lulach could see the remnants of the English army running for the hills. The ground was littered with bodies: dead and dying men, horses that heaved and struggled but would never rise again. There was blood everywhere, brighter than the heather, darker than the grass.

Lulach's horse was gone, cut from under him — how long ago he couldn't tell.

But they'd won.

It was a shock to Lulach to find himself still alive. Even more of a shock to realise that he could stop now, that no swords were slashing at him, no knives were stabbing at him. That he had space to look around, that he didn't have to fight every second to survive.

His arms hurt from wielding a sword, and he had a gash on one shoulder. His muscles screamed. His ears still rang with the sound of sword blows. But the clash of swords had gone. The field was silent, except for the moans of the dying.

A horseman cantered up to him, stepping between the bodies. 'Lulach!'

It was the King. His saffron cloak was stained with blood, but he seemed uninjured except for a gash on his cheek. He rode a different horse; Kenneth must have brought him another when his first horse fell. Or was this horse his third, or fourth?

'You're all right?' asked the King anxiously.

Lulach nodded, almost too tired for words.

Another man on horseback approached. Kenneth, his half face dripping sweat. 'An incredible victory, my Lord!' Only one side of Kenneth's face could show emotion now, but it glowed with triumph.

The King shook his head, gazing out at the ruin of broken bodies upon the field. He spoke almost without emotion. 'You never win a war like this. You only win a battle, for a time. Some things must be fought for over and over again.'

Lulach looked around. Only three of Macbeth's guards still had their horses. Perhaps some had given theirs to the King. Tiredly he began to work out who was safe, and who had died . . .

But they'd won, they'd won. Impossible to think of anything more, except . . .

Lulach turned to Kenneth. 'Where's Knut?' he asked urgently.

Kenneth shook his head. His eyes were kind but full of sadness. 'I'm sorry, lad.'

'Where is he?' demanded Lulach again.

Kenneth waved down into the glen. 'Somewhere ...' he said.

Lulach handed Kenneth his sword. He began to trudge down the hill, between the bodies.

How did you know who was alive and who was dead? Open eyes, staring at the sky ... Open eyes meant death. But others were sprawled among the heather, their faces to the ground.

The world was all dying men and treeless hills. The sky was still bright. That's the trouble with summer, thought Lulach hazily. The days are so long that night never comes.

'Water!'

Lulach kneeled. The boy was young. You needed to be twelve to join the army, but many boys lied about their age — or never knew it to begin with. Lulach held his water skin to the boy's lips. He seemed unhurt, if you didn't notice his blood-soaked cloak, the shadows in his eyes. Lulach beckoned to a stretcher party to come to the boy's aid, then he walked on.

And then he found him.

Knut lay near the body of his horse. It was easy for a man on foot to cut a horse's hamstrings, to bring it down. Horses never survived a battle long. An army needed many horses to replace the fallen.

Lulach kneeled by his friend's body. For a moment he thought Knut was dead. Then the bruised eyes opened. 'Have we won?' Knut whispered painfully.

'Yes, my friend.'

'Good.'

Around them Macbeth's men collected spears and hunted out the enemy wounded among their own.

'I'm dying,' breathed Knut.

Lulach tried to find words of reassurance. But he owed his friend the truth. The blood that seeped onto the ground was black, not red.

'Yes,' he said.

They had both made their confessions and been shriven before the battle — afterwards there were never priests enough. There was nothing Lulach could do now but wait with Knut until the end.

There should be something you could say to a dying friend, thought Lulach. Words of love, or comfort. But his body and his mind were numb. Words wouldn't come.

So he sat there, Knut's hand in his, till Knut's breathing stopped. Even then he stayed there, too numb with grief to move.

A thousand years later, Luke waited too, refusing to struggle out of his dream. Knut would never know that two sat with him, not one. It was all that Luke could do for Lulach. Lulach would do the same for him, he thought vaguely, if he had to sit like this with Patrick . . .

'My Lord?' It was one of the King's guards. 'The King wants you.'

'I'm coming.' Lulach placed Knut's hand on his bloody chest. 'Stay with him,' he ordered. 'I want his body taken home for burial.'

It was the last, the only thing that he could do for his friend: to take him home.

Home, thought Luke, restless on his pillow. I *am* home. I'm not really here . . . there . . . The smell (

blood, the scream of a wounded enemy seeing a knife come down ... None of it can touch me. I'm here in bed.

Then suddenly the dream was gone.

Luke half awoke. For a second he wondered where he was. Here or there; battlefield or bed?

But he was home. He was safe.

No — how could he be safe after a battle like that?

But it was Lulach's battle, not his ...

So that's what it's like, thought Luke, to fight for your country. To fight and win.

Exhaustion claimed him — exhaustion from the battle, from living it, or dreaming it. He slept again. But his dreams were normal now: faces that vanished a moment after they arrived, things that didn't matter flickering by.

How long he dreamed like that he didn't know. And then the chaos steadied. The world grew clear again.

The other world, a thousand years ago.

Time blurred.

Somehow Luke knew that three years had passed for Lulach. Years of hunger, as once again the country tried to recover from the loss of so many men. Years of arming men for war and raising armies. Lulach was a man now, not a youth — a man who'd lived through three years of war.

Because Malcolm had attacked again.

No one had won this battle. Both armies were destroyed.

The King knew that if Malcolm attacked again, with more mercenaries from Ireland, the battered Alban forces wouldn't be able to repel them.

They needed yet another army. And there was only one place where they would raise one, a place where every man was loyal to their mormaer. Moray. This time even the old and sick, the cattle herders in the farthest glens, were needed.

Now, as Luke dreamed, Lulach galloped north with the King and his guard. This time the north would rise against the enemy.

This time, maybe, they'd win.

The track was muddy, and there were trees and mist around them. The air smelled of distant snow, but Lulach was hot from hard riding. The sweat ran down his back and under his leather jerkin. They'd reach the monastery of Aboyne tonight, before crossing the mountains to their own lands.

The horses were panting, their breath white in the cold air. The King raised a hand, then pulled his own horse around. 'We'll stop here awhile!'

Macbeth had aged, Luke realised, as he watched the King lead his horse over to a well just off the track. His red hair was flecked with grey, his face creased with weariness and trouble.

The well stones were covered in moss. Above them bare crags rose grey as the clouds. The air was thick and still.

Lulach dismounted. One of the guards pulled up the bucket from the depths of the well. The King drank first, then Lulach. The horses would drink later, when they were cooler. Cold water now might give them colic.

Lulach gulped the water gratefully. It tasted of ancient rock and soil.

There were oatcakes in his saddle bag, and cheese. One of the guards pulled out a slab of dried fish.

'You and your fish farts can ride behind me, then!' joked one of the younger guards.

The King gazed at the sky. 'Storm before nightfall,' he said with a frown.

'We'll be at the abbey by —' began Lulach.

But Kenneth interrupted him. 'My Lord!' He pointed urgently down into the mist.

Then Lulach saw them too: riders, far below them, galloping hard, a flash of helmet and armour. Then they vanished again, into the trees.

'Malcolm's men,' said the King flatly. Men on horseback were rare. Men with swords and armour even fewer.

Lulach felt a cold certainty settle into his bones. 'Malcolm couldn't defeat the King in battle,' he said. 'So he'll ambush him where no one can see.'

Facing your foe in battle was honourable. But only a coward or a criminal ambushed an enemy.

'How many?' asked the King crisply.

'I counted four,' said Lulach.

'I'd say ten,' said Kenneth. 'More, perhaps.'

Lulach stared at the trees below, but their branches hid the riders. Could the King's party escape? he wondered. Their horses were tired. But the English horses might be tired too.

Kenneth made a quick assessment. 'We're safer meeting them head-on than having them at our backs. My Lord, you and the lad go across country, with two guards. I'll lead the rest to intercept them. That'll give you time to get away.'

'No,' said the King softly.

'But my Lord —'

'I won't send a man to any battle that I won't face

myself. You and Lulach head across country. Make for Aboyne as we planned; they'll give you sanctuary there.'

'Father!' protested Lulach, then hesitated. What could he say? 'No, this is too dangerous'? The King knew the danger as well as he did. 'You ride to the Abbey and let me fight in your place'?

He met his father's eyes — tired eyes, the eyes of a man who had done his best, done better for his people than any king before him.

But it had not been enough.

And the King was right. If they both died, Malcolm could seize the throne before an election could be held. But if the King was murdered here today, every man in Alba would rise to fight for his son.

His father smiled. He hugged Lulach quickly, then stepped back. 'God go with you, my son,' he said quietly. 'Look after Alba and her people. Tell your mother . . .' He paused. 'Tell her . . .'

What? thought Lulach. Praise her for her duty, her loyalty? Praise her for the years she has spent governing Moray in your place, while you have led the country?

But instead the King said softly, 'Tell her that in her I've had my earthly joy.'

The King strode to his horse and mounted swiftly. Within seconds his horse's hooves were pounding down the track, his guard following behind.

Kenneth swung himself into the saddle. The unscarred half of his face was grim; the scar blank, as it always had to be, emotion burned from it. But these days Lulach hardly saw the scar.

'Hurry, my Lord!' Kenneth urged.

Lulach nodded.

Their horses cantered up the hill, their hooves striking sparks against the rock. His father had kept him safe, again . . .

His father . . .

Memories came crowding in. The day his father was crowned king, hoisting him up onto his shoulders.

His father in battle, putting his shield and body in front of the sword that would strike his son down.

His father . . . not the King . . .

Suddenly Lulach pulled on his reins. The horse jerked around.

'My Lord!' yelled Kenneth.

'I'm going back!' shouted Lulach.

'But the King ordered —'

'And now his tanist gives you other orders! Follow me!'

Back down the hill they galloped, into the trees again, back to the track, their hooves thundering against the ground.

Lulach could hear the clash of swords now. Then he and Kenneth were on them.

Four, ten . . . no, fifteen invaders, one horse dancing free, its rider already on the ground. They must have hoped to catch the King unawares, rather than fight his bodyguard.

Fourteen of the enemy, then, against twelve of them. We can do it! thought Lulach, as he added his yells to Kenneth's and waved his sword above his head. This is our home ground; the land will give us strength . . .

There was no fear now, no confusion.

Each battle is easier, thought Lulach, urging his horse towards the King.

And then there was no time to think. His body took over, and his sword arm — thrust, parry, thrust again — his horse, thank God, steady beneath him, unfazed by the clash of battle . . .

One guard down, blood welling at his neck. Two of the enemy crumpled on the ground. The guard had sold his life dear. A scream as another horse stumbled — theirs or the enemy's, Lulach couldn't tell.

Slash, parry, slash again, sparks rising as iron smashed into iron.

The sound of hooves again: one of the enemy, galloping away. A second following, and then a third . . .

We have them on the run! thought Lulach triumphantly, as his opponent twisted at his reins and galloped off.

The King sat straight in the saddle, his eyes wide. Safe! thought Lulach exultantly.

Then the King's mouth opened. Blood flowed out, bright as a bird in the morning.

'Father!'

But the King no longer saw. He fell from the saddle, his fingers still clasping the reins. Then the fingers opened. The King lay upon the ground, a knife between his shoulder blades.

Lulach leaped down and stumbled towards him.

'The coward!' cried Kenneth hoarsely. His scarred cheek had been slashed open. Blood flowed freely onto his shirt, but he made no sign that he felt it. 'He must have stabbed him from behind.'

Lulach said nothing. He kneeled at the King's side.

'Father!' he whispered.

The King stared unseeing at the sky. But his lips moved. 'Tell them I did my best.' And then, so soft it almost wasn't there, 'Remember me.'

Had he really heard it? The blue eyes were sightless now. There was neither breath nor life.

The King looked smaller suddenly. It was his strength that made him large, thought Lulach blankly.

'Should we go after them, my Lord?' cried Kenneth.

'No,' said Lulach. 'They'll make for the border now.'

'But we must avenge the King!'

I have been a boy, thought Lulach. Now I must be a man.

The guard waited for his orders. Not just the guard, he realised, but all of Alba. They're mine to care for now.

'There'll be revenge,' said Lulach slowly. 'But not today. Not when we're tired, and they can ambush us again.'

Sweat blurred his sight. Blood dripped from his forehead. Years of battles stretched in front of him, against an enemy who could afford to pay anyone who'd fight for gold.

'You were a king of peace and plenty,' Lulach whispered to the man on the ground. 'You've left me to be a king of war.'

How could he bear it?

Chapter 26

Lulach

My name's Macbeth.
(*Macbeth*, Act V, Scene 7, line 7)

How could he bear it? Luke struggled desperately to wake up.

'No!' He tried to form the words, but his lips were numb. He had to wake up! It couldn't be like this! He had to escape — into daylight, the modern world with Mrs T's muffins on the table and the smell of coffee.

But the dream held him tight.

The scene blurred around him. The voices faded, the scents of blood and metal. The trees vanished.

There was another smell now, salt. The scream of seagulls, sea spray upon his skin. A deck heaved under his feet. Somewhere, sailors were singing as a lone piper played.

Where was he? What had happened? Where was the King?

And then he knew.

This was the King's last voyage, as they carried his body across the sea to his final resting place, with Alba's other leaders on the holy isle of Iona.

The wind blew from the island, bringing with it the song of dead kings.

'Remember me . . .'

'We won't forget you, Father,' whispered Lulach. 'They'll sing of you for a thousand years.'

Were the clouds weeping too? The mist came lower and lower still.

But it wasn't mist, Luke realised. The dream, the ancient world, was vanishing.

The story had ended.

His dreams had begun when Lulach's father died. Now they would end with Macbeth's death. Whatever happened to Lulach, somehow Luke knew that the dream would never come again.

Chapter 27

Luke

The day almost professes itself yours,
And little is to do.

(*Macbeth*, Act V, Scene 7, lines 27–28)

It was a shock to find himself in his bed in the silent house.

'Please don't end it yet!' Luke begged. He wanted to see the funeral, the nation weeping for their king, the holy rites on the cold island, the mourning . . .

'It's my right!' he whispered. 'I was there. I was with you. I saw it all!'

But he was a thousand years and half a world away.

They did remember you, he thought. Lulach was right. You were remembered for a thousand years.

But as what? Not Macbeth the hero. Not Macbeth the ruler of Alba's golden age, with his wife, the calm, the dutiful Queen Gruoch. They remember you as a coward and a villain, and your wife as a mad and scheming woman with bloody hands.

Lies, thought Luke. The world remembers lies.

Lies matter, he told himself. How could I ever have thought they didn't?

His pyjamas were wet with sweat, as though his body had fought those ancient battles too. He lay shivering for a moment, then got up. Dawn was a blur through the curtains.

'Lies killed you,' he said to the dead king. 'Malcolm lied. King Edward lied. They lied and said you had no right to the throne, because you were elected, not the son of a king. The English changed your history.

'Now all that's left is a lie too.'

Why me? he wondered. Why did the dream come to me?

Because I've been thinking about lies? Because I wanted a stepfather like Macbeth, a man I could admire? Or was there something more?

There was no way he could go back to sleep. He dressed quickly, then went out to the kitchen.

Sam was already there. He gestured at the kettle. 'Like a coffee? I'm just having a quick cup before I head out to the airport.' He grinned. 'I reckon I've just got time to get down to Sydney, get the make-up on and start talking. Let's hope there's no hold-up with air traffic control.'

'What if there is?'

Sam shrugged. 'I've prerecorded stuff. Not as good as doing it live, but it'll do.'

'Sam . . . please can you help the Fishers?'

Sam put down his coffee. 'Luke, I explained —'

'But you can try! Please! Please, Sam.'

Suddenly he was so angry it was almost impossible to speak. Why couldn't he have had a stepfather like Macbeth, someone who had the courage to do what was needed no matter what cost to himself? But instead he had Sam, more like Malcolm than Macbeth — Malcolm the liar, Malcolm the thief, just like Sam had stolen Mum and their lives and the farm. And now he knew what to say.

'Some things are important! Some things are worth fighting for!'

Where had the words come from? Megan, or his dream? It didn't matter. They were his words now. 'What sort of person can't fight for what he loves?'

Sam looked at him strangely. 'It means that much to you?'

'More than anything,' said Luke passionately. And it was true. 'Megan would be great on TV. She really knows how to say things ...'

Sam sipped his coffee. Thinking of another excuse, thought Luke. But, to his surprise, finally Sam nodded. 'Luke, I can't promise anything. But if it means so much to you — well, I'll see what I can do.'

It was all he was going to get. But somehow Luke knew that he really meant it. Sam would try.

Suddenly his anger evaporated, leaving emptiness and something else too. Awkwardness? A small bit of conscience as well? Because Sam *did* try.

'Thanks,' said Luke. 'Thanks for ... for everything. And for looking after Mum too.'

'Hey,' said Sam a little self-consciously, 'it's my pleasure, mate.' Then, as though he wanted to sweep the emotion from the room, 'You're up early. What's up?'

'Assignment,' said Luke. 'Due in today.'

'Hard one?'

Luke shook his head. 'Not now.'

It was true. He had to change everything he'd written. He might lose everything today. Not just his scholarship, but his friends too. Patrick. Megan.

He was risking hurting Mum as well. But Mum would cope. At last he knew what he was going to say.

Lies killed Macbeth. Lies were poisoning his own life.

Now he was going to tell the truth.

Chapter 28

Luke

But screw your courage to the sticking-place,
And we'll not fail.

(*Macbeth*, Act I, Scene 7, lines 61–62)

'Lady Macbeth wasn't evil,' concluded Megan. 'She was trapped. It was her duty to help her husband, who was too much of a coward to do what he wanted without her pushing him into it. Like him, she was trapped by the witches. But most of all, she was trapped by the time she lived in.'

Luke began the clapping. The rest of the class followed. Mrs Easson clapped too. She looked amused. 'Fascinating,' she said as the clapping died down. 'Very good indeed. You've reminded us that there's more than one way of looking at this play. Luke?'

Luke stood up. His knees felt funny, as though one of Macbeth's witches had turned them into marshmallow. *Double, double toil and trouble*, he thought vaguely, make Luke's legs begin to bubble.

It seemed to take an hour just to get to the front of the classroom. The faces swam before him.

Suddenly it seemed like the whole class was just one face.

For a moment he felt too scared to speak. What was he doing? They'd laugh at him ... Then Megan grinned and mouthed, 'Good luck!'

Luke nodded, and began to speak.

'"Macbeth's Progress into Villainy".'

His voice squeaked. Someone giggled. Luke took a breath and tried again. 'This is supposed to be how Macbeth was corrupted by the witches and went bad. That's what you wanted, wasn't it?' he asked Mrs Easson.

Mrs Easson looked startled. 'This is your assignment, Luke.'

'But teachers know what they want when they ask kids to do assignments,' argued Luke. 'There was lots of stuff on the Internet I could have used, really high-mark stuff. That's how it's supposed to go, isn't it? You steal other people's ideas and put them into your words and you get high marks for it? But I'm not going to.'

'Luke ...' said Mrs Easson. 'I think you need to answer the question.'

'I'm going to,' said Luke. 'But I'm going to do it in a different way. I'm going to tell the truth.'

'Get on with it, man!' muttered Jingo from the back, fiddling with the notes of the talk he'd given earlier. Luke ignored him.

'Once there was a king of Alba called Duncan. Alba was what they called ancient Scotland. Scottish kings were elected in those days, like we elect people to Parliament and they elect the Prime Minister.

'But King Duncan kept fighting wars to expand his territory. People were starving. So the chiefs and churchmen elected the Chief of Clan Moray as king instead.

'Outside Scotland royal families poisoned each other and made war. But things were pretty good in Scotland. The new King united the whole country for the first time. He made sure everyone followed the laws. Scotland was a place where the old and sick were protected, and where women had equal rights. Everything was peaceful and prosperous.'

'What's this got to do with Macbeth?' This time Jingo's voice was louder.

Luke ignored him and went on.

'But the dead King's son, Malcolm, had fled to the English court. The English didn't have the same sort of laws as Scotland. The English didn't elect their kings either — the king's son became king no matter how stupid or bad he was. So the English King helped Malcolm raise armies to conquer Scotland.

'But Malcolm's armies couldn't take Scotland. So Malcolm sent assassins to murder the Scottish King.'

Luke looked out at the class. They were all staring at him, trying to work out why he was telling them all this. 'The Scottish King's name was Macbeth.'

'But Macbeth was a bad guy!' objected Jingo.

'No, he wasn't. The Irish and Norwegian and Scottish historians said Macbeth was a really good king. Only the English historians said he was a bad guy. And then six hundred years later Shakespeare wrote his play.

'Shakespeare made Macbeth even worse. He added witches, because King James hated witches. He made Banquo look really good, because Banquo was one of King James's ancestors. He made Macbeth's wife into

195

a madwoman, even though the real person was known as a really wise queen.

'Shakespeare didn't care what was true,' said Luke. 'He only cared about sucking up to the King.'

'Luke, this isn't fair . . .' began Mrs Easson.

'Isn't it?' demanded Luke. 'I asked you two days ago, "How can Shakespeare have written all that when it wasn't true?" and you said it didn't matter. That the play was more important than the truth.

'Well, I don't think it is. Does truth matter? I think it does. What if someone wrote a play in a hundred years' time about our prime minister? How he was so evil he secretly murdered all his opponents? Or how he was so brave he fought off the New Zealanders when they tried to invade?

'Neither one would be true. But people might think it was true . . . especially if it was a brilliant play.

'Shakespeare didn't have to write about a real king. He could have written about, oh, King Jason, if he'd wanted to. Someone who never existed. But Shakespeare didn't just want to write a brilliant play. He wanted money and a licence to perform from the King. So he lied.'

'So what?' It was Jingo again. But for once he looked interested. He wasn't just objecting for the sake of it. 'What does it matter if some old guy lied, like, a hundred years ago?'

'Four hundred,' put in Mrs Easson.

'Whatever. Who cares?'

'Because truth matters,' said Luke slowly. 'If someone in a hundred years' time writes a play about you, for instance, and says you were, I don't know, a wuss or something, would that matter?'

'Man, I'd bash his —'

'But you'd be dead! There'd be nothing you could do!'

'But does it *matter*?' asked Megan suddenly. 'In a hundred years' time, what does it matter if people think Jingo was a wuss or not?'

'Hey, it matters to me!' called Jingo.

'That's what I've been thinking about for the last week,' said Luke. For longer than that. For ages.

'What does it matter if Shakespeare lied? What does it matter if people lied about weapons in Iraq?

'Everybody lies these days. Most ads on TV are just a lie. I thought: maybe lies are okay if they lead to something good.

'But are they really?

'I think lies are wrong. When you lie about something that matters ... well, you know you've done the wrong thing, that's all.

'Maybe lies are wrong because they're so easy. A company doesn't have to make an iceblock that tastes better than everyone else's. They just have to *say* it's better. Or a government can hire people to say it cares about — oh, not having enough hospitals or something, without really doing anything about it.'

Luke paused. The class was quiet.

'Maybe lies are wrong because every time you find out someone has told you a lie you trust other people just a little bit less. And if people can't trust each other, well, how can we keep working together?'

He took a deep breath. 'I sat the exam for St Ilf's Grammar last month. And they gave me a scholarship. But I wrote a letter this morning refusing it. Because I'd already seen the questions on the exam paper. I didn't mean to cheat — they must have sent me the exam paper accidentally, with some old ones.'

Everyone was staring at him. Even Mrs Easson. Even Jingo. Luke tried to read Megan's expression, but he couldn't.

What were they all thinking? He couldn't tell. But he had to go on.

'I wasn't a cheat then. But I would be now if I kept the scholarship. I'd be a liar. I'd always know that I'd been wrong.'

Suddenly he had run out of words. He looked at the notes in his hand. There was one more thing he had to say.

'Some things are important. Some things are worth fighting for. Truth matters. Because if we don't tell the truth we don't just cheat other people. We cheat ourselves. How will we live if we don't know what's true, or who to trust? If our friends ... or our leaders ... or the people we admire lie to us?

'It's not easy sometimes to tell the truth. Sometimes it's not easy to hear the truth either. But we need to try. And ... and ... if my great-grandson wants to write a play about a wuss, he'd better not call the hero Luke.'

His legs were marshmallow again. Swords would have been easier, he thought vaguely. You know where you are with swords.

What now? He'd lost the scholarship. Probably no one here would ever speak to him again, and that'd really matter now that he had to stay here for the rest of school.

He was halfway to his seat before he noticed the applause.

Chapter 29

Luke

Will all great Neptune's ocean wash this blood
Clean from my hand?

(*Macbeth*, Act II, Scene 2, lines 59–60)

Luke sat down in his seat, trying to get his breath back. Patrick turned round and gave him a thumbs up. Over by the window Megan was grinning.

'Well done, Luke,' said Mrs Easson. She looked a bit stunned, as though she wasn't sure if she was congratulating him for his honesty or his talk. 'Excellent. Really excellent.'

It was over, thought Luke. Or was it? He glanced at Megan.

No, it wasn't over yet. One lie down, and one still to go. He had to tell Megan that Sam couldn't — wouldn't — help.

He *had* to tell her, as soon as English was over . . .

Someone knocked on the classroom door. 'Message for Megan and Patrick Fisher. They're wanted at the office.'

Mrs Easson nodded. 'Off you go, Megan, Patrick.'

What was wrong? Were their parents okay? Luke peered out the window as Patrick and Megan hurried along the verandah and up towards the office.

'Well,' said Mrs Easson, 'I don't know if any of us will be able to concentrate after that. But we do have some more talks to get through . . .'

It seemed an age before English finished. Luke gathered his books together as his classmates passed him one by one.

'Good on you, Luke.'

'Yeah, mate. Well done.'

'Thanks,' muttered Luke. He didn't know what else to say.

Half of his mind was on Megan and Patrick. Were they okay? What was going on?

Now they'd all gone except Jingo. 'Hey, Luke!'

'Yeah?'

'Did you really refuse the scholarship?'

Luke nodded. 'I posted the letter before school.' He frowned. 'I haven't told Mum and Sam yet.'

Jingo was silent for a moment. Then he said, 'I don't think I'd have been able to do what you did today. It took guts.'

'Thanks, Jingo,' said Luke, touched.

He followed Jingo out of the classroom.

There was no sign of Megan or Patrick on the bus. No one knew where they'd gone either.

The house was empty when he got home. Mrs T would be out getting the groceries today. There was a note from Mum on the bench, where she knew he'd find it when he looked for something to eat.

> *Gone to Sydney with Sam. Back tonight.*
> *Love, Mum.*

Luke opened the fridge and took out a carton of milk. There was the rest of last night's chicken there too. He'd grab something to eat then ring the Fishers ...

Just then the phone rang. Luke put the chicken back and picked up the receiver.

'Luke?' It was Megan. Her voice was ... different. Excited.

'What's wrong? Is everything okay?'

'Everything's wonderful! Turn on the TV!'

'What —'

'Have to go! I want to watch it too! Just wanted to say thank you! Thank Sam for me too!'

'What —' The phone went dead.

Luke raced over to the TV and switched it on.

Cartoons. Why would Megan want him to watch cartoons?

Unless it was something on another channel. Luke switched them frantically, barely noticing what he was doing. Why hadn't she said which one?

And suddenly there she was, on the screen, in the Fishers' orchard, with her parents and Pat behind her.

'I ... it's been ours for over a hundred years,' she was saying. 'Some things are important. Some things are worth fighting for. It's not just our farm that's threatened. It's anyone who is growing food that people need, running a family business, people like us coming up against big companies that can force them out. People need to know that they can rely on their council or their government to protect them. People need to know who they can trust.'

My words, thought Luke. Megan's using my words.

The scene changed. It was the Mayor. He looked harassed and embarrassed and defensive. 'Certainly no decision has been made ... Environmental considerations are always important ...'

'Then you don't think this resort will be approved?' The interviewer wasn't Sam. It was a woman.

It's a different station, Luke realised. Not Sam's at all.

The Mayor gulped, staring at the camera. 'Of course, I can't make a decision myself. That's for the Council. But if I were a betting man I'd say it was very unlikely.'

The interviewer turned to camera for the wrap-up. But Luke wasn't listening. He had to thank Sam, apologise to him ... or something. He picked up the phone again and dialled Sam's mobile.

'Hi, you've called Sam Mackenzie. I'm not here at the moment ...'

The answering machine. Should he leave a message? The beep went before Luke could think what to say. 'Sam, it's Luke. I ... I'll call back later.'

He turned back to the TV. The Mayor's face had vanished. In its place a shot of the Fishers' farm appeared, taken from the high point near the rock where he'd sat with Megan, while the program's credits rolled. It was a shock to see the rock like that, on a TV screen. It looked so different that it was almost as though he'd never seen it before.

How could he possibly have thought he could leave the farm and go to St Ilf's? He'd go to agricultural college eventually, perhaps spend a gap year who knew where. But Breakfast Creek was the heart of his life. His country.

And it had taken Megan to show it to him.

There was the sound of a car outside, then Mum's voice and Sam's in reply.

What was Luke going to say to them? What *could* he say?

'Luke? Are you there?'

'Here, Mum.'

'Oh, Luke.' Mum was carrying a giant pizza box. It was hard to read her expression. Sam stood behind her, holding a bag of groceries. 'The school called me a few minutes ago.'

'You mean St Ilf's?' But they wouldn't have the letter yet, Luke realised.

'No, it was Mrs Easson. She said you gave the most wonderful talk she's ever heard in all her years of teaching. Luke, I'm so proud of you.'

'Mum . . . I'm sorry about St Ilf's . . .'

Mum's voice was choked. 'I never wanted you to go away to Sydney anyway. Just to have a chance . . . the sort of chance your dad never had.'

'I've got all I want right here,' said Luke, without hesitating.

'Oh, Luke. Come here.' She hugged him hard. The pizza box began to crumple, sending a dribble of melted cheese down Luke's front. But it didn't matter. 'That stupid school, sending you the wrong paper . . .'

So Mum didn't know Sam had been behind it — even if he'd never meant it to go so far. Luke met Sam's eyes. Sam's face was carefully bare of expression.

No, thought Luke, Sam wasn't Malcolm, the thief, the betrayer. And if he wasn't Macbeth the hero either — well, who was?

Sam did his best. Which was more than most people ever tried to do, Luke realised. And today, at least, Sam's best had been pretty good.

'Thank you,' he said to Sam.

'Ah.' Sam's voice was suddenly ... what? thought Luke. Friendly? Normal, not the 'I'm on show' voice? Relieved? But sort of proud of himself too. 'So you've seen it.'

'Yes. It was wonderful! Was it you? I mean, did you ...'

'Just pulled a few strings,' replied Sam, and he definitely sounded proud of himself now. 'Still have a few contacts in the opposition. They did an okay job, didn't they?'

'Yes,' said Luke. So did you, he thought. But he didn't say the words. He didn't need to.

'I'll just put this in the oven,' said Mum tactfully, as she tried to smooth out the crumpled pizza box. 'Celebration tonight! Oh, blast the thing, it's all gooey. Well, maybe we can go out. The Fishers might like to come too.' She took the groceries from Sam and disappeared into the kitchen. She was humming again.

'Luke, mate, I'm sorry,' said Sam. 'You know I didn't mean —'

'It's okay,' said Luke. And if Sam hadn't exactly said what he was sorry for, well, that didn't matter either. Because it *was* okay. 'And I really like the bike,' Luke added.

This time Sam's grin was genuine. 'Hey, mate, maybe I should get another one for me to ride too. By the way,' he added, almost too casually, 'I've put in a bid for the resort land. Guess they won't be wanting it now. Might get it cheap. Thought you and I could sort of toss around a few ideas about what we might do with it.'

'Wagyu cattle,' said Luke automatically.

'Way what? Look, mate, we'll talk about it tonight, okay? I need to go get changed out of my city clothes.'

There was a pause, then Sam said, 'We did good today, didn't we? You and me?'

'Yeah,' said Luke. 'We did good. Thanks, Sam.'

'Thank *you*, mate,' said Sam. He hesitated, as though he were going to hug Luke too, but didn't quite know how. He slapped his back instead, and headed off to change his clothes.

Chapter 30

Luke

Peace! — the charm's wound up.
(*Macbeth*, Act I, Scene 3, line 36)

It was warm on the rock, despite the wind's cold breath on their cheeks. It was as though the rock had sucked in the summer's heat and stored it for them till winter.

Megan's legs dangled over the edge next to Luke's. 'So you're not going to St Ilf's?'

Luke grinned. 'Nope. The Headmaster wrote a letter back, saying how I'd been so honest that they'd still like to have me. But I want to stay here.'

'For *To-morrow, and to-morrow, and to-morrow*,' quoted Megan. '*To the last syllable of recorded time . . .*'

How much of that play has she memorised? thought Luke. He could only remember a few lines.

Weird chick. But nice weird. At least he understood what she was talking about.

'I'm glad you're staying,' said Megan. '*Really* glad, I mean.' The look in her eyes was one he'd never seen there before.

'*I'm* glad I'm staying too,' said Luke.

How would she react, he thought, if I kissed her? He put his arm around her, felt her lean towards him.

It didn't quite work out as he'd expected. Her lips were warm and really soft, but he could have done with an instruction manual — like a tractor manual, but for kissing. How long was it supposed to last?

But it was still a bit of heaven.

They said nothing for a while. Who'd have thought it? Luke wondered vaguely. Would those two little kids playing Explorers all those years ago ever have imagined they'd be here one day doing this? He'd never thought he could feel like this ... but at the same time it was almost familiar too. I feel like Lulach did when he met Thora, he realised. My heart's been filled, and I never knew that it was empty.

What would Lulach have thought of this world? he thought suddenly. Or Shakespeare?

'*Life ... a tale Told by an idiot, full of sound and fury, Signifying nothing.*' No, thought Luke. Shakespeare's words were great. But he was wrong. Life was good, very good.

'It's a great play, though,' said Megan, as though they'd been talking about it all along. Her arm was around him now too.

'Yeah,' said Luke, surprised. 'I was just thinking that.'

'Those lines of Lady Macbeth's ... *all the perfumes of Arabia will not sweeten this little hand,*' she quoted.

Megan had nice hands, thought Luke. They'd done things. Pruned trees, turned pages ... 'You really like all that stuff, don't you?' he asked.

Megan grinned. It was a bit like Thora's grin in his dream. 'Yep.'

'Even though Shakespeare lied?'

'Sure. He was a brown-nose *and* a great writer.'

They both laughed.

Maybe Sam's like that, thought Luke suddenly. Not good, not bad, but a mix of both.

'You know what?' said Megan.

'What?'

'I'm going to write a play about Macbeth one day. But a true play, not a lie.'

'Seriously?'

'Yeah. We need to remember things. Like how a lie can become the truth for four hundred years.'

An eagle circled down to look at them, wondering if they were small enough to eat, then soared slowly up above the valley.

Finally Megan asked, 'Did the St Ilf's Headmaster say who'd given you the exam paper?'

'Nope,' said Luke. He shrugged. 'Maybe it was an accident.' Or maybe it wasn't, he thought. But that was the Headmaster's business.

Things were okay with Sam now. He made Mum happy — and she liked looking after him. Luke just hadn't worked out that it was that way around before.

Sam had bought the land from the resort people too. Luke suspected Sam had wanted to give it to him; he'd heard Mum in the kitchen telling Sam firmly, 'Not until he's twenty-one!'

Sam was up for some award at the Logies this year. Luke and Mum were going down to watch, and Luke would get his first dinner jacket for the night.

Suddenly he had an idea. 'Um . . .' he said to Megan.

'Um, what?'

'Would you like to come to the Logies? Sam's up for an award.' He crossed his fingers, hoping that Sam could get another ticket.

'Hey, really? Cool.'

Luke supposed she meant yes. Maybe Sam could get two extra tickets, so Patrick could come as well. It was going to be a bit difficult, Luke thought suddenly, going out with the twin sister of your best friend . . .

'So,' said Megan at last, 'do you think the dreams will ever come again?'

He'd told Megan about the dreams too. It felt good to be able to talk about things like that.

'No.'

'How can you be so sure?'

'Dunno. I just am.'

'Why did they happen to you, do you think?'

'I don't know that either!' Luke grinned. 'I'm glad they did, though. But now it's the end.'

Megan smiled as Luke took her hand. 'Unless,' she said, 'it's the beginning.'

The dream had gone. The past had vanished. But the future looked very good indeed.

Epilogue

Lulach

... And all our yesterdays ...
(*Macbeth*, Act V, Scene 5, line 22)

Two men — one young, one old with a scarred face —
stood in a room that smelled of beeswax candles,
and beef smoke from the roasting ox outside.
In another room down the long corridor, the clan
chiefs and churchmen had sat for seven days to elect
their king.

Soon Lulach would address them for the last time
before their final decision.

Lulach turned his back on the grey sky showing
through the window. 'Do you ever dream?' he asked
his companion suddenly.

Kenneth looked startled. 'Of course.'

'Sometimes I have strange dreams,' said Lulach
hesitantly. 'I'm in a foreign land. A dry land, with
trees like ghosts rising from the grass ... There are
machines too. Powerful, almost like magic ...'

'It sounds like a nightmare,' said Kenneth.

'No. It's a safe land. No armies. No clash of swords.
No one looks hungry. No one is in rags. For a while I

thought I'd made myself a dream world where I could escape from being the King's son.'

Kenneth's half face smiled. 'I can understand that.'

'But I was wrong,' said Lulach. 'There were battles to be fought there too. Last night — in my dream — I was a boy again. And I promised . . .'

'What?'

'I promised I'd tell the truth. And I did. I got up before my friends and I told the truth. It doesn't seem like much of a battle, does it? Not as glorious as fighting the English. But just as hard. Because there was only me to fight it. Just one boy. I didn't have an army on my side.'

'Dreams,' said Kenneth dismissively. 'What use are dreams?'

'Who knows?' said Lulach softly. 'Nonetheless, today I'll tell the chiefs the truth.'

'Lulach MacGillecomgain Macbeth, Mormaer of Moray.' The herald's call echoed down the corridor.

Lulach stood up. Kenneth stood up too. Lulach embraced him.

'God go with you, lad,' said Kenneth.

Lulach stepped out into the corridor. No candidate could bring his men beyond this point. He was to be judged on his own merits.

A young man walked down the corridor towards him. He wore silk and velvet, not the wool cloth of a Scottish lord. His hair was cut in the English fashion.

Malcolm MacDuncan, thought Lulach.

This was the second time he had met the person who killed his father, he realised. Once he had met Thorfinn, the man who had sent his father home a twisted and blackened corpse. Now here was the man who had sent the assassin who killed his stepfather — though to Lulach, Macbeth would always be his father too.

Thorfinn had slain an enemy in battle, but Malcolm had struck like a cattle thief in the night. He hadn't even had the courage to do the deed himself.

What did you say to your father's murderer?

But there was no proof. There never would be, not for a thousand years.

'We meet again, Lulach MacGillecomgain,' said Malcolm. His voice was hoarse — a battle leader's voice, rough from shouting orders in the field. He spoke with a strong English accent.

'Your pardon. We've never spoken,' returned Lulach. But they'd met on the battlefield, hadn't they? he realised. And in its way, this was a battle too.

Malcolm looked at him appraisingly. When I'm king, he seemed to say, will you be loyal?

Because of course the chiefs would elect Malcolm. If they didn't, Malcolm would keep fighting with the power of England behind him, till he took the kingdom.

'Your pardon,' Lulach said again. The lords were waiting for him. Malcolm smiled slightly as Lulach left him.

It was a big room, and dark despite the torches on the walls. The windows were too narrow, the stone walls too thick, for the misty daylight to penetrate.

Lulach looked around him. For a moment the faces blurred. What were the chiefs thinking? That he was too young? That he was nothing like his stepfather? How could such a young man possibly rule Alba, much less lead it to war?

And then his vision cleared. He knew them all now: MacKinnon and MacPherson, Dunegal's son and Morgan the Red and all the others. He had known them all on the battlefield. He'd fought side by side with some of them. Others had been with Malcolm.

What could he say?

My stepfather would know how to move them, thought Lulach.

Macbeth would have told the truth.

He'd have used it like a weapon. And that weapon, at least, he had passed down to his stepson. The weapon that boy had used in his dream last night . . .

Lulach took a deep breath and faced the men before him.

'My lords,' he began, 'you gave my father a starving, wartorn country. He gave you back a golden age. We are a small nation. But my father made alliances with Thorfinn, with France, even with Rome. He was able to do that because men trusted him. All Macbeth had to give was his word. But it was enough.

'Today Malcolm promised you peace. He promised to keep the law of Scotland. But can you trust him to keep his word?

'How many times has Malcolm lied?'

There were murmurings in the crowd at that. They want me to say I'll lead them to victory, thought Lulach. Then they can cheer and pretend for a while that we'll win.

'I can't tell you that we'll win,' said Lulach softly. 'I wish I could. All I have to give you is my word. I promise that no matter what, I will tell you the truth. I promise to keep the laws of Alba. I promise that while my body still has blood and breath I'll do my best.'

There was silence for a moment.

And then the cheering started.

Perhaps tomorrow I'll be king, thought Lulach. 'Win or lose,' he whispered to his stepfather, 'I'll be an honest one. Rest in peace, my lord.'

Postscript

Lulach MacGillecomgain was elected king after the death of his stepfather Macbeth in 1057. He successfully held off the English (the histories don't agree on how long) until he, too, was murdered by Malcolm's men. King Lulach was buried with full honours on the island of Iona, as all Alba's kings had been before him.

Malcolm 'Big Head', who had murdered two elected Scottish kings to gain his throne, took over the land at Lulach's death and ruled until 1093, when, like his father, he was killed in one of the many wars he had started, this time against England.

From Malcolm's time onwards Scottish kings inherited their throne and weren't elected. The laws of Scotland that gave equal rights to women, that protected the poor, and many other laws that we think of as 'modern', were abandoned. Malcolm was buried at Dunfermline — the first king of Scotland not to be taken to the sacred island.

And sevyntene wyntyr full rygnand
As king he wes than in till Scotland
All hys tyme wes grete plente
Abowndand bath in land and se
He wes in justice rycht lawchtfull
And till hys legis all awful

And for seventeen winters he [Macbeth] *reigned*
As king, till Scotland
Had great plenty both in land and sea
All through his reign.
He kept to righteousness and the law
And his men loved and respected him.

From Andrew of Wyntoun, *The Orygynale Cronykil of Scotland*, written some time between 1395 and 1424. Author's own translation.

Author's Note

Macbeth was High King of Alba, or ancient Scotland, from 1040 to 1057. It's difficult to trace his true story. Most of the information that has come down to us was written by his enemies, and no two histories agree on what happened or when. (We don't even know if his hair was red or yellow.) I've chosen the most likely bits of several of them, but there are many possible interpretations of the patchy records.

All the histories make it clear, however, that Shakespeare's play was more fiction than fact. Much of it was based on the *Chronicles of Scotland* of Raphael Holinshed, who didn't understand ancient Scottish laws, and wanted to please those in power. Holinshed definitely made Macbeth a villain. But Shakespeare's Macbeth was far worse even than Holinshed's. Given that King James, the English king at the time of the play, was descended from Banquo and King Duncan, and had a particular hatred of witches, it's likely that Shakespeare deliberately changed history to please the King, just as he had changed historical details in earlier plays to gain favour from Queen Elizabeth I.

Even today, many history books are based on the English historian Holinshed, not the earlier histories. You'll read how Malcolm won the second battle against Macbeth — which doesn't make sense. If Malcolm won, Lulach couldn't have been elected king and crowned at Scone. Even a recent TV documentary about Macbeth didn't mention the Celtic laws, the fact that Alban kings were elected, or even that Malcolm only became king after the death of Lulach.

(The ancient Celtic laws are fascinating, and well worth studying. They also show the sophisticated ancient Scottish and Irish societies that were destroyed by war and invasion.)

Like Luke in this book, I think we owe a duty to the past. Which is more easily remembered: a historical story, play or film; or the words of a history book?

Historical fiction is a window to the past. But it has to be as true as you can make it — not a historical lie. When you write historical fiction, you have a responsibility to slip your fiction into the cracks in the historical record, not change history for your own ends, unless you make it clear that this is what you're doing.

This is what I've tried to do with this book, and my others. And where I've failed, well, like Macbeth MacFindlaech and his stepson Lulach MacGillecomgain, I've done my best.

Notes on the Text

Abbey gong: In a land with no watches and few clocks, one of the abbeys' many roles was keeping the time in their districts.

Arrows: Arrows were valuable. Only an expert 'fletcher' could make an arrow that went straight. An arrow fired by an expert bowman could reach about a hundred metres.

Bagpipes: The Scots first used bagpipes in battle in 1314, long after Macbeth's battles, but Irish mercenaries were using them around Macbeth's time.

Boot Hill: Called that because the chiefs carried the soil of their lands in their foot bindings up the hill, and so brought some of their homeland with them. They emptied the soil from their binding onto the Hill at coronations as an act of allegiance as they swore loyalty to the new king.

Clans: Alba was divided into six provinces, made up of different clans, or tribes. These weren't the same as today's Scottish clans, with their tartan kilts. The modern clan system evolved in Victorian times.

Claymore: A large sword, with an edge on both sides. It could be swung in one hand, while the other held a pointed shield that could be used as a weapon too.

Clothes: Men and women wore much the same clothes: smocks, or léines. Women's were longer; men's were shorter and worn over woollen stockings. Most léines were made from linen (imported from Ireland) rather than wool. Macbeth and Lulach may have worn silk léines, with red or gold embroidery. Usually only rich people wore bright colours, as it took a lot of work to dye cloth and most dyes soon faded, so clothes had to be dyed over and over again to keep their colours bright. Both men and women also wore cloaks, or brats, held in place with a pin or brooch.

Neither Macbeth nor Lulach would have worn a kilt. The first real evidence of kilts is in the fifteenth and sixteenth centuries, when long 'belted plaids' (blankets, or pleated garments) were worn over the shoulder, like a cloak, or belted at the waist.

Dirk: A long thin dagger.

The death of King Duncan: There are two main stories about the death of King Duncan. The later, English one is that Macbeth treacherously killed Duncan when Duncan was in Moray territory. The other (the version used here) is that the army of Macbeth and his Norse allies fought Duncan's army, made up mostly of his Atholl clansmen and Irish mercenaries. Macbeth won and Duncan was killed in the battle. I have assumed that the council of chiefs had already asked Duncan to step down, and that he had refused. If the council hadn't agreed with Macbeth's actions, they would never have elected him.

Fire: In a world without matches, wealthy people carried a 'tinderbox'. It held a flint, a bit of iron, and 'tinder' (wood shavings or dry grass). You struck a spark with the iron and flint and hoped the 'tinder' caught alight. But most homes kept a fire smouldering all the time, rather than keep trying to light one.

Ingeborg: Thorfinn's wife Ingeborg may have married Malcolm after Thorfinn's death. As Thorfinn was so much older than Malcolm, his first wife would also have been much older than Malcolm, so in my story I've made Ingeborg (or Ingibjorg) Thorfinn's much younger, second wife.

Language: The people in this book spoke Gaelic. I've had them talk modern English, as though I had translated directly from the Gaelic, rather than sprinkle modern Scottish words throughout the book.

A length: Distances were measured in lengths. A 'length' was the length of a horse.

Lulach: There is no record of who Lulach married, but it was probably an alliance with someone like Thorfinn's daughter. Lulach had one or two sons and a daughter. His son Melsnectai became Mormaer of Moray, but was banished by Malcolm and later became an abbot. The other son may also have been mormaer at one time, and Lulach's daughter's son, Angus, became mormaer as well.

Macbeth: Macbeth's real name was probably MacBheatha. 'Mac' means son, though we know

Macbeth's father was called Findlaech, so by then 'MacBheatha' was possibly a name in its own right. Findlaech had been Mormaer of Moray before Lulach's father, Gillecomgain, was elected. Macbeth's mother, Doada, was probably the daughter of King Malcolm II.

Marriage by proxy: Often royal couples who lived far apart were married with someone else standing in for the bride or groom. That way they didn't have to risk having their bride or groom die or change their mind while they were on their journey, leaving them without any status in their new country.

Moray: Moray, or Moireabh, meant 'seaboard settlement'. It was the largest province in Alba, and was much bigger than the modern county of Moray.

Mormaer: A mormaer was a chief, elected by the people of a clan to rule them. (Even ancient Scottish fishing crews elected their captain, then agreed to obey him totally as long as he *was* captain.) Anyone who was related to the previous mormaer could stand for election, even a distant cousin. Women could be elected too, though this was rare. The chiefs in turn elected the king. By Macbeth's time kings were usually elected from Atholl or Moray, the two most powerful clans.

Chiefs and kings nominated their heir, or tanist, and trained the tanist to rule after them. A tanist still had to be elected by the people or the chiefs, after the mormaer's or king's death. But mostly the appointed tanist was elected — after all, they had been trained as an apprentice leader.

The king or mormaer had to follow Scottish law, which had been brought over by the colonists from Ireland. If he displeased the chiefs he could be asked to resign — just as the chiefs had to resign if they displeased their people.

Most disputes in Alba were settled by arbitration — both sides had to agree that the solution was just. So the king and chiefs had to be legal experts as well as leaders.

The Orkneys: The islands off the north of Scotland, held in those days by Thorfinn, son of Sigurd 'the Corpulent'. The Orkneys were cold, windy islands, but they controlled a rich fishing and whaling trade. They became part of Scotland in 1471.

Raths: Raths were like small villages, with a main hall, outbuildings and cottages, but where everyone usually ate at the hall. Sometimes everyone slept at the hall too, but in other places most people had their own tiny cottages. A larger rath might be a *dün*, or fortress.

St Ilf: There is no St Ilf or any school called St Ilf's. I deliberately used a nonexistent saint so no one would think the school in this book is based on a real school, or that the cheating episode ever happened. Nothing in this book is based on any living person, TV show, or school . . . certainly not any that I've ever been associated with.

Scotland: In Lulach's day Scotland was known as Alba, though it was beginning to be called by the Latin name Scotia, from the Irish *scotti* or 'skirmishers' who had settled there. Alba had been settled early in the third century by colonists from northeast Ireland, who intermarried with the Picts already in Scotland. Their language, Gaelic, was still the main language in Lulach's time, and Irish laws were still in force. Most of the people were fishermen, farmers, or cattle herders.

No one owned land. Instead, on the Feast of Nabach (from *Nābaicheachd*, meaning 'neighbourliness'), everyone drew lots to see what bit of land they'd farm the next year. Some of the land was kept to support the sick, old and poor.

Eating Like Macbeth

In Macbeth's time there weren't great differences between the way rich and poor people ate. In the Scottish halls everybody ate from the same big pot — the poorest person had the same food as the leader of the clan. I've assumed that when Macbeth was king he and his court ate in the English and European fashion, sitting at tables and eating from big trenchers of bread, with two people sharing a trencher. (Only the king and other important people had a trencher to themselves.) But as far as I know no one at the time wrote down how the Scottish court ate, so maybe Macbeth and his court kept to their old ways.

A clan's wealth mostly depended on how many cattle it had — and stealing your neighbour's cows was almost a sport. The female cows were usually kept for their milk, butter and cheese, not for meat. But apart from the best bulls, all male cattle were killed before they were a year old; it took a lot of hay to keep a cow through the cold winters. They were either eaten fresh at a feast, or dried or salted to stop the meat from going bad before it could be eaten.

Wild deer, hare and birds like partridges, grouse or mallards were also hunted and eaten. But meat was pretty much food for feasts and celebrations.

Instead of meat, most people ate a lot of fish and shellfish from the coast or the lochs (lakes). The fish were either eaten fresh, or dried, salted or smoked to preserve them. Many days of the year were religious 'fish days' too, when no one was allowed to eat meat. Cheese was another staple food.

Root vegetables like parsnips, swedes and white turnips were grown, as well as hardy kail (kale), which was a bit like an ancient cabbage. 'New' vegetables like leeks, onions, broad beans, radish and garlic may have reached Scotland by Macbeth's time too. Women gathered wild berries and wild greens like nettles, sorrel and syboes (spring onions), as well as edible seaweeds. The yellow turnips eaten with today's haggis didn't come to Scotland till the eighteenth century. The other modern Scottish staple, potatoes, hadn't come to Scotland in Macbeth's day either.

Wheat, oats and barley were grown in the more sheltered areas, but most places were too cold and windswept, so people traded cattle for grain from the south. Scotland had the earliest known water-powered mills for grinding oats and other grains into flour, and they probably existed in Macbeth's day, though most households would have had their own small 'quirm', a mortar and pestle, for grinding their own grain.

Oats and barley were made into porridge by grinding them and boiling them with water. Often everyone ate the porridge from the same pot, dipping their cow's-horn spoon in to get some porridge then dipping the spoonful of porridge in milk or cream, sometimes sweetened with honey, or in butter. Porridge was also cooked with kale or wild herbs. A drink called brose was a bit like a very thin porridge, and another drink called sowans was made from fermenting oat husks in water.

Most cooking was done in a single big pot in the fireplace. Meat and fish were roasted over the fire on a spit, and oatcakes or bannocks were baked on the hot hearthstone by the fire (there were no ovens in ancient Scotland). Barley or oat bannocks were large, soft and round. Oatcakes were harder and thinner, and could be dried in front of the fire so they'd keep for weeks or months when you were travelling, or out fishing, or at war. Special hard oatcakes of oatmeal and butter were made for babies to cut their teeth on, like modern rusks. Salty oatcakes were made at Halloween; if a young man or woman ate one they were supposed to dream of whom they'd marry. Special soft oatcakes made with cream and honey (and later sugar) were made for celebrations when a couple was married or a baby was born.

Oatcakes
- *2 cups of rolled oats, or oatmeal flour if you can find it in a health-food shop. If not, grind the oats to flour the traditional way, between two rocks. (Wash the rocks well first!)*
- *half a tablespoon of salt*
- *2 tablespoons of butter*
- *a little cold water or buttermilk*

Mix the oatmeal flour with the butter and salt, then add a dribble of cold water or buttermilk and mix again, and keep adding dribbles of water till the dough is moist enough to form a ball.

Use your hands to take small bits of the dough. Roll each one into a ball, then press it as flat as you can and place it on a greased oven tray. When all the dough is used up, put the tray into a cool oven and bake at about 100°C for 40 minutes to an hour, or till the oatcakes are firm and just starting to turn pale brown.

Eat them hot or cold with lots of butter and cheese. If you want to store them, leave them propped up by the fire for several days till they are very hard and crisp.

Brose

- *2 tablespoons of rolled oats*
- *1 cup of cold water, meat stock or buttermilk*
- *cream and honey, or butter*

Cover the rolled oats with the liquid and leave for an hour or two. Then mix them into the liquid with a spoon or your fingers.

Strain out the lumpy bits. Add a dash of cream and honey, or heat up the brose and stir in a lump of butter until it melts.

Kail Brose

- *1 cup of chopped kail (kale) or cabbage if you can't get kail. (You can buy kail seeds in Australia, but it can be hard to buy the leaves.)*
- *1 litre of water or beef stock*
- *1 tablespoon of oatmeal*

Simmer the kail in the stock till soft. Put the oatmeal on a tray in a hot oven till just pale brown, which should take about three minutes. (It would have been browned on the hearthstone in Macbeth's day.) Serve the soup in bowls and scatter the toasted oatmeal on top just before you eat it.

Green Cheese

Green cheese wasn't coloured green. It was a fresh cheese that could be eaten after a couple of days. Other cheeses were made into 'hard cheese' that would last for months or years.

- *1 litre of milk, yoghurt or whipped cream*
- *1 junket tablet (optional)*
- *a colander*
- *some very clean cloth*
- *string*

Leave the milk in a bowl, covered by a cloth, till it thickens. If you are afraid it may go bad in our hot climate before this happens, use a junket tablet to thicken it instead according to the directions on the packet. This will take a couple of hours. Or use yoghurt or whipped cream instead, which are already thick.

Line the colander with the cloth. Pour in the thick milk. Leave it for about an hour then gather the edges of the cloth together and tie them with the string. Hang the wet bag somewhere cool where all the liquid dripping out won't make a mess. (I hang mine from the tap in the bath or from the shower.) Leave it till all the liquid has run out and it feels firm. This will take between two and four days.

Unwrap your cheese and keep it in the fridge till you need it. Eat it as it is, or on oatcakes. You can also eat it with fresh or puréed fruit. (I like mine on crackers with Vegemite — definitely not known in Macbeth's time.)

Clotted Cream

The thick cream we eat today is mostly whipped. Lulach and Macbeth would have eaten clotted cream on oatcakes or wheat bread, or with wild berries.

Take a bucket of milk fresh from the cow. Leave it on the hearthstone by the fire for a day and a night. The cream will rise to the top, and get firmer and thicker. When it's so thick you can almost slice it, scoop it off.

Butter

Lulach and Macbeth would have eaten a lot of butter, either on oatcakes or barley cakes or in their porridge. The easiest way to make butter today is to half-fill the bowl of an electric beater with cream, then just keep beating till the cream separates into lumps of butter and thin 'buttermilk'. Use a couple of spoons to press the buttery lumps together and press out the buttermilk. (Too much buttermilk in the butter quickly turns it sour.)

If you want to store your butter for a few years, pack it into a wooden bucket, put the wooden lid on firmly and bury it in your nearest cold peat bog or swamp.

Jackie French is a full-time writer who lives in rural New South Wales. Jackie writes fiction and non-fiction for children and adults, and has columns in the print media. Jackie is regarded as one of Australia's most popular children's authors. Her books for children include: *Rain Stones*, shortlisted for the Children's Book Council Children's Book of the Year Award for Younger Readers, 1991; *Walking the Boundaries*, a Notable Book in the CBC Awards, 1994; and *Somewhere Around the Corner*, an Honour Book in the CBC Awards, 1995. *Hitler's Daughter* won the CBC Younger Readers Award in 2000 and a UK National Literacy Association WOW! Award in 2001. *How to Guzzle Your Garden* was also shortlisted for the 2000 CBC Eve Pownall Award for Information Books and in 2002 Jackie won the ACT Book of the Year Award for *In the Blood*. In 2003, *Diary of a Wombat* was named an Honour Book in the CBC Awards and winner of the 2002 Nielsen BookData/ Australian Booksellers Association Book of the Year — the only children's picture book ever to have won such an award. More recently, in 2005 *To the Moon and Back*, which Jackie co-wrote with her husband, Bryan Sullivan, won the CBC Eve Pownall Award for Information Books and *Tom Appleby, Convict Boy, My Dad the Dragon* and *Pete the Sheep* were also named Notable Books. Jackie writes for all ages — from picture books to adult fiction — and across all genres — from humour and history to science fiction.

Visit Jackie's website

www.jackiefrench.com

or

www.harpercollins.com.au/jackiefrench

to subscribe to her monthly newsletter

OTHER TITLES BY JACKIE FRENCH

Wacky Families Series

1. My Dog the Dinosaur • 2. My Mum the Pirate
3. My Dad the Dragon
4. My Uncle Gus the Garden Gnome
5. My Uncle Wal the Werewolf
6. My Gran the Gorilla
7. My Auntie Chook the Vampire Chicken (June 2006)
8. My Pa the Polar Bear (January 2007)

Phredde Series

1. A Phaery Named Phredde
2. Phredde and a Frog Named Bruce
3. Phredde and the Zombie Librarian
4. Phredde and the Temple of Gloom
5. Phredde and the Leopard-Skin Librarian
6. Phredde and the Purple Pyramid
7. Phredde and the Vampire Footy Team
8. Phredde and the Ghostly Underpants

Animal Stars Series

1. The Goat that Sailed the World (August 2006)

Outlands Trilogy

In the Blood • Blood Moon • Flesh and Blood

Historical

Somewhere Around the Corner
Dancing with Ben Hall and Other Yarns
Soldier on the Hill • Daughter of the Regiment
Hitler's Daughter • Lady Dance • Valley of Gold
How the Finnegans Saved the Ship • The White Ship
Tom Appleby, Convict Boy
They Came on Viking Ships

Fiction

Rain Stones • Walking the Boundaries • Summerland
The Secret Beach • Beyond the Boundaries • A Wombat Named Bosco
The Book of Unicorns • The Warrior — The Story of a Wombat
Missing You, Love Sara • Dark Wind Blowing
Ride the Wild Wind: The Golden Pony and Other Stories

Picture Books

Diary of a Wombat • Pete the Sheep
Josephine Wants to Dance (November 2006)

Non-fiction

How the Aliens from Alpha Centauri Invaded
My Maths Class and Turned Me into a Writer
How to Guzzle Your Garden • The Book of Challenges
Stamp, Stomp, Whomp (and Other Interesting Ways to Get Rid of Pests)
The Fascinating History of Your Lunch
Big Burps, Bare Bums and Other Bad-Mannered Blunders
To the Moon and Back • The Secret World of Wombats
How to Grow Your Own Spaceship (February 2007)